A BASTARD FILE

A Novel

Mark Starr

A BASTARD FILE

A Novel

Mark Starr

Railroad Street Press
394 Railroad Street, Suite 2
St. Johnsbury, VT 05819

Published in the United States by Railroad Street Press, St. Johnsbury, Vermont.

ISBN: 9780984473885

Library of Congress Control Number 2010931427
    1.   Fiction

Jacket design by Mark Starr

First Edition 2010

Railroad Street Press
394 Railroad Street, Suite 2
St. Johnsbury, VT 05819
(802) 748-3551
www.railroadstreetpress.com

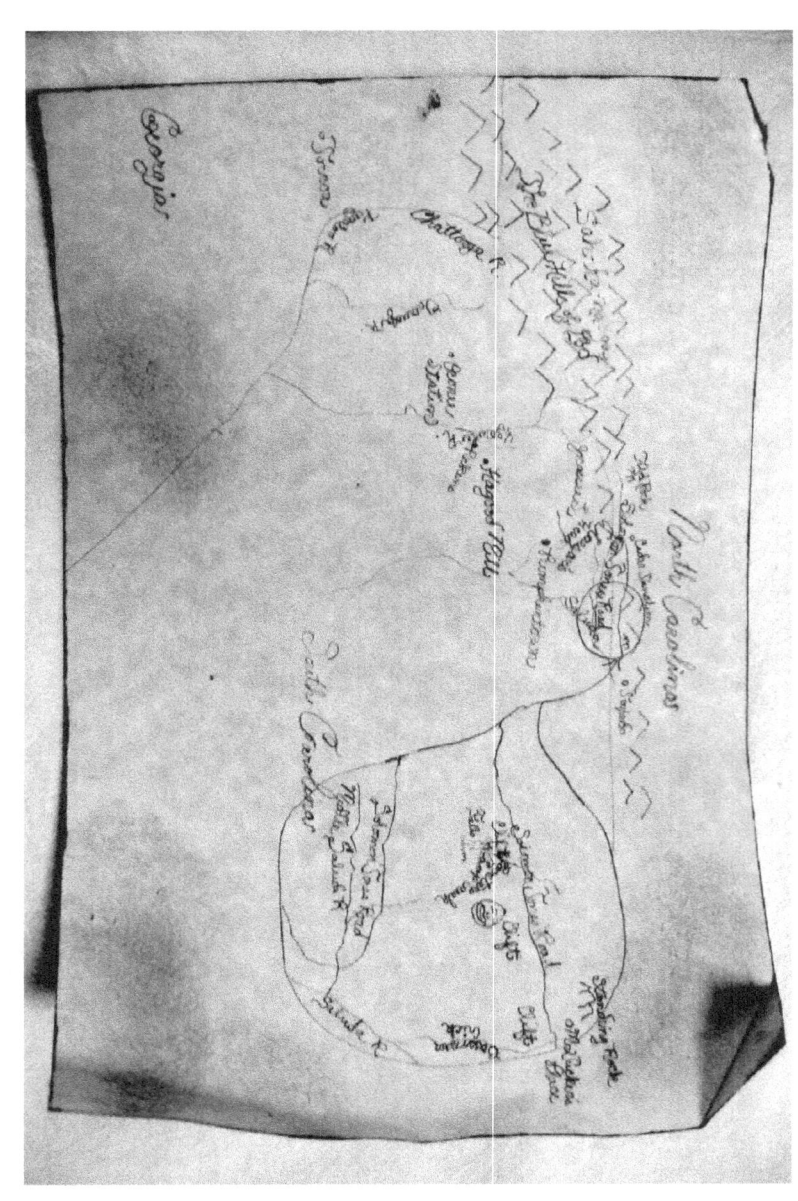

Authors Note:

The families written about in this novel are fictional but some of the background events and characters of the nineteenth century were actual ones. Around 1830, there was a gold rush in Georgia, and Benjamin Parks is generally attributed with having made the find which sparked it. Templeton Reid was an enterprising individual who ran one of the private mints in the area. I took liberties with the dates of operation of his mint, but there is enough truth in what was written about his coins that you may want to consider numismatics as a hobby.

I did not inspect the root documents, but a review of secondary sources leads me to believe that the State of Georgia enacted anti-Cherokee laws as generally described. General Winfield Scott was assigned to move the Cherokee peoples west, to land now in Oklahoma (it was not yet a state), and Tsali is honored in Cherokee tradition. Aptly, the forced relocation would come to be known as the Trail of Tears, for thousands are believed to have died before reaching their new home.

PROLOGUE

Autumn, 1828

THE SOUTHWEST PORTION of the Blue Ridge Mountains was Cherokee Territory. Deer were plentiful here, but Ben had been in the woods for hours and had yet to see one. He was worried, fearing that without more venison they would not survive the coming winter. Had he seen movement through the trees? He froze in his tracks and held his breath. *Yes.*

Stealthily, Ben moved forward to get a clear shot, but then he stepped on a twig. Snap! His prey bounded away. *Blast!* Ben gave chase, even though he knew it was hopeless.

Running through the woods at full speed, he caught his foot under a fallen branch and plunged forward with an "uumph." Instinctively, he dropped his rifle and his arms flew out to keep his nose from hitting the ground.

He didn't immediately get up. Instead, on hands and knees, he dropped his head and grieved the loss of the deer; a big one, judging from the racket it made when making its escape. And then he saw it: a big rock jutting from the ground about where his head would have hit had he not succeeded in breaking his fall. *Whew.*

He looked at the rock more closely. The rock held shiny golden chunks embedded in quartz. *Can't be.*

Not wanting to return home empty handed, he decided to lug the rock back to their cabin. On the way, he bagged a wild turkey, lifting his spirits. Ben tied the turkey's legs together with a cord and slung it over his shoulder. With the added burden he was tempted to discard the rock, which seemed to grow heavier with each step, but he couldn't bring himself to do it.

Finally, he caught sight of a wisp of smoke—coming from their cabin's chimney he reckoned. *Almost home!* After about ten more minutes of arm-lengthening travel he heard his wife's whistling. It cheered his soul. *Must be hangin' out the laundry.* He let out a shout.

"Hey, the cabin!"

Announcing one's coming was an expected courtesy in these parts. Without it, a visitor might receive the dubious honor of a shotgun salute.

As he entered the small clearing his wife smiled and said, "Hey back," but she continued to string wet clothes on the line. She had no time for socializing; there were chores to do.

Ben lifted the cord holding the turkey's legs from his shoulder and hung his prize from a peg on the wall of their shed. *I'll get to him later*, he decided, not relishing the job of plucking and cleaning the bird. Many men he knew considered this women's work, but a lesson his mother taught him as a child had stuck with him: "You kilt it, you clean it."

Still carrying the rock, he walked toward his wife, glancing at the lye tub to see whether it was time to add more ashes from their fireplace. Soaking the ashes produced the lye they needed to make soap and hominy, and while he could do without the first, he was partial to the latter. Having taken his eyes off where he was going, he almost stepped on a hen busying herself with some cracked corn. The hen's squawking and fluttering startled him.

"Tarnation! That's twice in one day I 'bout planted my chin in the dirt."

His wife tried to hide a chuckle.

Recovering his composure, Ben paid close attention to his feet as he closed the gap.

"Say, what d'ya make of this?" he asked, displaying the rock.

"I reckon that there's what's callit a rock."

Peeved at his wife's sarcastic disinterest, he persisted. "I done toted this spec'men two mile. Least you could do is 'zamine it."

So she did. The golden chunks could not be missed. "Benjamin," she said earnestly, "I'll clean the bird whilst you take that there gemstone to town."

Ben did as he was told, and luckily found someone who knew something about mineralogy.

News of Benjamin Park's discovery spread rapidly, drawing thousands to northeast Georgia.

America's first gold rush had begun.

CHAPTER 1
SHOCK AND AWE

"HEY, AARON, what does 'sultry' mean?"

Aaron stopped and wet his lips with the last drops remaining in his water bottle before answering. "Just like you to be dreamin' about girls when all I can think about is putting one foot in front of the other."

"Huh? I thought the word had to do with the weather." Kyle looked confused.

"Well, you're the scholar, but I thought it was the kind of eyes some sexy lady sitting in a bar has. You know…sultry eyes."

"Oh, yeah." Kyle looked uncertain.

The brothers were hiking back up from a little known waterfall nestled in a small box canyon about halfway down the Blue Hills escarpment, an imposing steep ridge which creates a natural border between North and South Carolina in the mountain-west region of the two states.

The trail to the falls was not an easy one. After dropping off the shoulder of the highlands, the trail became so steep that their pace on the way down was almost as slow as this hike back up. But the effort came with rewards. It had been a fine sight, watching the water spout like a cliff diver from an unknown source over a hundred feet above, plunge down through a rainbow mist, and then explode upon the granite slabs at its base. Though they stood about thirty feet away, the cool spray had wafted over the teens, giving them much needed relief.

However, for the past half hour or so they had been doing some steep uphill scrambling and the only thing now dampening their tee shirts was hot sweat. With the heavy humidity, high temperature and motionless air, the conditions were downright miserable.

"What's say we take a break? This is as good a place as any." Aaron plunked down on a tree-shaded rock ledge and removed his ball cap to release the steamy heat. Kyle collapsed beside him.

Aaron used the back of his forearm to wipe away the sweat that streamed from his forehead and stung his eyes, and then he turned to Kyle. "Can I have some of your water?"

"Sorry, I'm empty, too." Kyle added a probative shake of his water bottle.

Aaron shook off his backpack and swung it around to his lap. Then he rustled through the contents to fish out a big Fuji apple, his favorite variety. "Here, this ought to help some."

Kyle accepted it with a grin, freeing Aaron to hunt for another. Soon they were both chomping away, obviously relishing every drop of the sweet and tangy juice which trickled into their dry mouths and throats.

"D'ya suppose they ship these things all the way from Japan?" Aaron asked after a while.

"Why would you think that?"

"Fuji... I think it's the name of a volcanic mountain over there."

"Nah. They may have come from Japan to begin with, but now Fuji apples are grown here; I saw some last fall when our class took a field trip to the apple farm over by Etowah."

"Still, darned good eatin'."

"Yup."

After another couple of bites Aaron burst forth in song. "Nothing could be finer than a Fuji apple in Caroliner in the mo-o-orning!"

"Oh, puh-leaze....spare me," Kyle pleaded.

"You're just jealous because you can't sing."

Aaron wished he could snatch the words back. When Kyle was in second grade, something happened that had cut the boy deeply. His class was rehearsing its winter program. Kyle was belting out the chorus when his teacher interrupted the song to suggest he simply mouth the words. Of course, news of it quickly spread through the school. Despite their parents' efforts at damage control, Kyle had not sung a note since.

Kyle made no reply. Shame and regret silenced Aaron, too. They just sat there with their elbows propped on their knees, looking down at the ground while nibbling away at their apples.

When he had reduced his to its core, Aaron began to toss small rocks off the trail. As he watched one bounce toward the lip of a rocky outcropping several feet to his left, his eyes locked onto something out of place; something with straight lines and the look of gunmetal.

"What's that?" he wondered aloud.

"Where?"

Aaron got up and shuffled across the narrow rock ledge to a place the outcropping widened and then bent down to pick up the object. It was a steel file about ten inches long and one inch wide. There was no handle; just an exposed prong, or tang.

Except for a small, red stain on one side, it looked new. He sidestepped back to where Kyle was seated and showed him his find.

"Wonder what that was doing there?"

"Beats me," Aaron replied with a shrug. Doubting the owner would return to look for it, or find it if he did, he slid the file into his pack.

They resumed their upward trudge and within the hour had conquered the roughest part of the hike. Sorely needing water, they debated where to get some. Kyle proposed that they fill up at the nearby youth camp but Aaron didn't want to go there. It was uphill, in the wrong direction, and he had qualms about entering without an invitation. He preferred to take a chance on finding water at a nearby open air chapel perched along the rim of the escarpment. Maintained by the youth camp, the chapel was open to the public during daylight hours and Aaron was fairly sure it had restrooms and running water.

But when he suggested the chapel, a pleading whine exploded from Kyle: "Nooo! Let's not go there."

What got into him? Aaron had fond memories of the place and was glad to have an excuse to return. Their parents had taken them there for an Easter sunrise service once, and Aaron could still recall how his heart had swelled when the sun rose above the foothills at the same time as the worshippers stood to join the choir in celebration of their risen Lord.

And then he remembered. For Kyle, that Easter had not been a good one. After being roused out of bed at 5 a.m., he had to be forcibly dressed. Then he was nudged and shoved to the car through the pre-dawn darkness; all the while complaining that he didn't feel well. Aaron allowed as if he might have been telling the truth, too, for the poor kid had gotten sick in the car during the long roller-coaster drive to the chapel, and then had slept through most of the service.

Well, he'll just have to get over it, Aaron decided. "Look, I'm not riding my bike any farther than I need to when there's water at the chapel. You're supposed to do what I tell you, and that's where we're going."

"Alrighth," Kyle conceded grudgingly, his tongue sticking to his palate. He tried to spit the cotton out of his mouth but the spittle clung to his lip, creating a line of foamy drool to the base of his chin.

"Nice wad, bro!"

Kyle finished wiping it off with the back of his forearm and then punched Aaron in the arm, momentarily raising the pitch of Aaron's chuckling.

Soon their bicycles came into view. After Aaron unlocked the cable which secured the bikes to a tree, they mounted their steeds and pedaled down the paved road which dead-ended at the chapel parking lot. Coasting through the empty lot, they dismounted at the top of the chapel steps and within seconds were standing in front of the two restrooms flanking the covered entry.

Aaron reached for the doorknob to the Men's but stopped when he saw the door was padlocked. Sensing Kyle's glare on his back, he turned toward the Women's.

"You're not going to use the ladies', are you?" Kyle asked incredulously.

Aaron turned to look him in the eye. "Why not? There's nobody here."

Kyle shoved his water bottle at him. "Here, take mine; I'm not going in there."

Aaron rolled his eyes, took the bottle and grabbed the doorknob. *Oh, crap.* The door was locked. Aaron dropped his head and sighed. Now it looked like backtracking to the camp was their only option, and with an uphill bike ride to boot.

Suddenly the knob clicked and turned and the door swung open.

"We didn't know anybody was in there!" Kyle exclaimed in rapid-fire testament.

Aaron just stood there, fish-mouthed and wide-eyed, with his shoulders hunched to his ears and his arms and hands splayed like a gecko's.

Facing him was the most beautiful creature he had ever laid eyes on.

CHAPTER 2
LENA

ALTHOUGH THE GIRL standing in the doorway was vulnerably alone, it was obvious that the two fellows were more startled than she was. She giggled.

Aaron's hands dropped to his sides and his face lost its contorted look, only to be replaced by a crimson glow rivaling his brother's.

"Wuh….wutta you doing in there?" he blurted. It sounded like an accusation.

Stiffening, she retorted, "Why are y'all breakin' into a locked ladies' room?"

Aaron noticed that her eyes and area around her nostrils were red. "I, uh, I'm really sorry," he began sincerely, when he could speak. "We needed water and were trying to find a place to refill our bottles."

The girl gave a little nod and then extended her hand. "My name is Lena, what are yours?"

Whoa! The sight of her had already taken away his breath. Then she adds this delicious southern accent. *Is there such a thing as love at first sound*, he wondered? He shook her soft, slender-fingered, hand.

"Hi, Layna, I'm Aaron Gardner and this is my brother, Kyle."

She giggled again.

Now what did I do?

"It's Lena," she corrected, spelling it out as she freed her hand from his.

"Oh, *Lee*na, not *Lay*na," he replied, eliciting a nod.

"Pardon me for blocking the door," she said after a moment. "I'll move so y'all can get some water."

Aaron was blocking her way out, but he failed to take the hint, so Lena squeezed past him.

Without taking his eyes off of her, Aaron held out the water bottles in Kyle's general direction. "Here, Kyle, fill these up will ya."

"No way!" Kyle shunned the bottles as if they held toxic waste.

"Oh, I'm sorry. I can fill those for you," Lena volunteered.

With a girl present, Aaron didn't feel right about going into the ladies' room, so he was glad to relinquish the bottles.

Lena's fingers brushed against his when they made the exchange, causing his heart to race.

"Thanks," said a squeaky voice he didn't recognize as his own.

Although Lena was merely standing at the sink, Aaron felt awkward waiting by the open door, so he and Kyle moved into the chapel without walls. It was as Aaron remembered, its humble pulpit of cemented stones flanked by a simple wooden cross, and the most awesome backdrop: a sea of bluish hills rolling to the hazy horizon.

Shortly, a sweet voice came from behind them. "Isn't the view amazing?"

They turned to see Lena holding out their water bottles. "Thanks!" said Kyle as he grabbed his, and immediately squirted a stream into his maw.

"Yeah, thanks," added Aaron, reaching for one, too. The few minutes it had taken Lena to fill the bottles had allowed his heartbeat to slow to where he could no longer feel it pulsing in his ears. But now the sensation threatened to return, so he moved his focus from her eyes to his bottle…and the soft, exquisite fingers curled around it. *Help me, Lord*, he prayed, as his hand drew closer. Being ever so careful not to touch her, he circled the top of his bottle with his thumb and forefinger and gently slid it out of her grip. *What a wimpy move.* He checked her expression and was relieved to see a grin which seemed not to think less of him.

"Comin' Aaron?" called Kyle from the chapel entrance.

"In a minute." Aaron's voice was tinged with irritation. Never before had he wanted to get to know someone as much as he wanted to get to know this girl. He knew that if they left now there was little chance he would see her again. He turned to Lena and explained, "We're expected home for dinner and we've got quite a ways to ride."

"Aren't y'all staying at the camp?" she asked in surprise.

He explained that they lived near Hendersonville, a town several miles to the northeast, and had just come for a day hike to the waterfall.

"Oh." Lena looked and sounded disappointed.

"Have you seen it yet?"

"The waterfall?" Lena shook her head. "I didn't know there were any around here."

"You don't know about the waterfalls?" Kyle exclaimed, having bounced back down the chapel steps. "There's the one just below the camp…we could show you the trailhead if you'd like…the hike to it is pretty tough, though…and then there's Raven Cliff – it's over in South Carolina, but it's only a few miles from here, and there's Triple Falls, and High Falls, and…."

"There are quite a few in the area," Aaron interrupted, not knowing how long Kyle might rattle on. "Some of the nicest ones are in the state forest where our dad works. It's only about six miles from here, as the crow flies."

"Maybe we could take you to see them sometime," offered Kyle enthusiastically.

"I would really like that," Lena gushed. "Do you think we could go? I just love wattafalls."

Aaron smiled crookedly. He had no idea how they could. Neither he nor Kyle had a license to drive, much less a vehicle. But after hearing the joy in that silken voice with its heavenly accent he couldn't bring himself to disappoint her. Instead, he stood by silently while Kyle and Lena traded phone numbers.

Then, after a brief farewell, the brothers started for home, pedaling into the forest on an old logging road nearby. Before the road curved, Aaron braked to a stop and looked back through the tunnel of trees, hoping for one last glimpse.

His eyes dropped. She was not there.

CHAPTER 3
THE FACE JUG

Atlanta, Georgia
Sometime the previous fall

"IF DUST WAS WORTH something, I'd be a millionaire," he muttered to himself after a couple of hours rummaging through furnishings and keepsakes his wife had inherited. What he had seen so far consisted mainly of old unmatched dishes, cross-stitched dish towels, photo albums, crocheted doilies, gaudy costume jewelry, and boxes of 1950's vintage vases.

They had stored the items in their attic with the idea of going through them one day. That had been several years ago. After one too many of his get-rich-quick investments proved to be get-poor ones, he decided to tackle the project; some of the stuff might be valuable.

He hadn't told his wife of his plan. He feared she might not want to part with some whirligig once owned by Great-Great-Grandma Wheezy-Whatsername. Plus, he liked the idea of having his own little slush fund. *What she don't know won't hurt her*, he reasoned, and so he waited until he had the house to himself.

Today was the day. Their daughter was in school and his wife was at some "Save the World Dysfunction," as he liked to call them.

He wished he knew more about antiques. At times he pictured himself becoming rich when one of his precious finds was identified as a rare collectible but then he would return to earth and admit that he hadn't found anything he hadn't seen before at garage sales or thrift stores. Nevertheless, he pressed on, setting aside anything promising.

After building a substantial pile, he scanned the attic for a suitable container. His eyes settled on an old trunk. It had leather handles at each end, tin sides stamped with starburst patterns, and dark stained hardwood slats evenly spaced around the sides. *It might even be worth something, too,* he thought, as he ran his fingers across the name SADIE STREETER crudely etched into one of the slats.

It was not a name he recognized.

Opening the lid, he found the trunk divided into two compartments. In the larger one were a couple of stiff floral print dresses, some yellowed cotton undergarments, a small quilted blanket, an old leather Bible, a hair brush and hand mirror set with ornate silver handles, and a sepia photograph of a young woman holding a baby. The woman was seated at a table on which was displayed a framed photo of a confederate soldier proudly holding his rifle.

In the smaller compartment, padded by wadded newspapers from the late 1800's, was the oddest clay jug he had ever seen. It resembled an old moonshine jug, with a large base and a stubby little neck with a finger-sized handle. What struck him was that it had a sculpted face on one side. It was no ordinary face, either. Eyebrows had been made by slicing dozens of small slits in the mounds of clay built up at the base of the forehead. Eyeballs, complete with hollowed out moon-shaped irises, appeared to have been formed separately and then inserted into their sockets. Somehow the potter had shaped the nose so it appeared to be longer than it actually was. The most prominent feature, though, was the mouth. Creepily real-looking teeth were encased between its extraordinarily wide and thick lips. A few of the teeth were missing, but as far as he could tell, the potter had made it that way.

The presence of the teeth somehow made the face jug more lifelike, almost as if someone had breathed life into the clay. When he held it up and looked it in the eyes, he shivered.

The jug was corked, so he gave it a shake. Something rattled, but it wasn't liquid. He pried out the cork and peered inside. It was too dark to see anything so he turned it upside down and shook it, hoping the contents would fall out. But then he suddenly stopped. He saw that letters had been carved into the bottom.

"JULISDANALI," he slowly read aloud. He rotated the jug 180 degrees to see whether the writing made more sense that way. *Nope.*

He returned to shaking the jug.

When it became clear that this wasn't going to work, he stuck his little pinky into the opening to see if he could pin the object to the side and pull it out with his fingertip. After struggling with it unsuccessfully for a couple of minutes, he swung the jug against a sharp corner of one of the wooden posts. With a thud, the jug broke into pieces. "Wiped the grin off your ugly face now, didn't I?" he said with a sneer.

Lying amidst the shards was a rolled up envelope, yellowed with age. He picked it up and examined it. It appeared to be handmade as none of the seams were sealed and the flap showed no evidence of adhesive. It was addressed to "Sadie Williams Holton" of Georgia and had a North Carolina general delivery return address for "Mr. Samuel Tucker." It was written in beautiful cursive. He lifted the flap and leafed through the contents. *No cash. Dammit.*

He was about to toss the envelope on the floor but paused, and then stuffed it into his pocket, instead. Then he began to hurriedly load the trunk. There was no time to waste; his wife or daughter could return at any time and he didn't want to have to explain why he was home or what he was doing in the attic.

CHAPTER 4
JULISDANALI

Former Cherokee Territory
Circa 1830-1850

IN 1837 GENERAL WINFIELD SCOTT arrived in the mountainous region near the junction of Tennessee, the Carolinas, and Georgia with orders "to carry out the benevolent intentions of the United States Government" toward the Cherokee: moving them to lands set apart for them west of the Mississippi River, a journey of a thousand miles.

The following spring General Scott assembled the tribe's leaders and announced that every man, woman, and child of their peoples must be on their way before the waning of the next full moon. And if they weren't? In a not-so-veiled threat, he asked that they spare him from having to witness the destruction of the Cherokee.

Soldiers began to force the Cherokee out of their houses and off of their farms, moving them into stockades to await the long journey. Tribal tradition tells of one Cherokee who did not go quietly, a man named Tsali. Offended when one of the soldiers used his bayonet to prod his wife for moving too slow, Tsali crept to the man's tent one night and stabbed him to death. Tsali then assembled his family and fled, seeking refuge with other Cherokee who were hiding in the mountains of North Carolina.

Until then, General Scott had paid little attention to the fugitives. There were too few of them to pose much of a threat to settlers and he doubted anyone would raise a ruckus if they kept to the mountains; the land was too steep and too forested to be of much use. However, the killing of one of his men could not be ignored, so Scott sent one of the Cherokee in his employ to find Tsali and deliver this message: Surrender to be tried and we will ignore the others in hiding.

Tsali and his sons gave themselves up so that the fugitives could remain in their beloved Sah-ka-na-ga; the Great Blue Hills of God.

Tsali and all but the youngest of his sons were shot by firing squad.

Word quickly spread among the fugitives. It struck one of them especially hard. Not knowing that he was helping the military, it had been he who told General Scott's scout where to find Tsali. The hard realization that he had betrayed one who was willing to die that others might live free added one more link to the young man's heavy chain of sorrows.

His entire life he had witnessed many of the Cherokee doing their best to conform to the encroachers' ways. They had become farmers, raised livestock, built houses and barns, and even established businesses. They sent their children to missionary schools to learn to speak and write English. Despite all of this, they had been run off their lands and farms, which were then sold in a state lottery. How could this be when the federal government had guaranteed them this land forever, he wondered?

He had asked his uncle why justice was not sought from the white man's court. His uncle answered that the takers were shrewd; they had made a law which said a Cherokee could not sue a white man. "Then they should be made to answer in Cherokee court," he had countered. He could still picture his uncle, shoulders hunched and looking very tired. "The takers also have made a law that says we cannot have a constitution and laws of our own." Fists clenched and breathing hard, the youth had struggled to find words, but none came. He had run outside so his uncle would not see his tears.

Eventually, the persecution closed in. Because his mother was a Cherokee, he was fired from his job at a gold mine; the only job for which he had ever been paid. He had been good at it, too. He had a knack for finding placer deposits; places where fine grains of gold would collect as part of the sedimentary process. The mine's owner said he was sorry to let him go but that he had no choice; the Georgia militia had begun to enforce a state law prohibiting the employment of any Cherokee in mining operations. The pain of this injustice was multiplied by the knowledge that this once had been the Cherokees' homeland.

Life at home had also been difficult. His father, the owner of a trading post, treated him and his sister and their Cherokee mother more like property than kin. He never understood why his mother had taken up with the man; she must have known that any children of their union would suffer abuse. The youth had been accepted by the Cherokee, but this was not always true among the settlers. Had alcohol been the lure that drew her to the man and kept her chained to him? It pained him to think about it.

When they got wind of the Cherokee removal, his father declared that his business was worth more than they were; he was staying. The youth would never forget how his mother begged his father to keep their daughter, a frail eleven-year old, to spare her the long and rigorous journey. Nor would he forget how his father refused.

It was then the youth stopped using his given name of James Streeter. In its stead, he took the name he had been called by his classmates at the missionary school he attended as a child: Julisdanali, the Cherokee word for "catfish". His classmates had been poking fun at his wide mouth and thick lips, but with the passage of time the name had lost its sting.

All these things weighed upon Julisdanali, but when his mother gave his sister to a childless couple who had won some of the Cherokee lands in the lottery, he could bear no more. But for this, he may have gone to the western territory with his mother and his uncle. *No*, he decided, *family is too hard a thing. I will stay in the Blue Hills. If I die, I die. At least my body will rest where it belongs. Starvation, cold, weariness; these are all things I can endure. But the sickness of my heart is too heavy for me. It is better if I do not go.*

Word of the Cherokee fugitives had reached the trading post and Julisdanali ran away to join them. Venturing alone, but helped along the way by sympathizers, settlers and Cherokees alike, he succeeded in reaching their hideout in the rugged and wild mountains.

He found that the band consisted mainly of those who had the least. Unlike those who had adapted to white civilization, they had retained their hunter-gatherer skills and could survive more readily in the forested mountain habitat. Following their example, Julisdanali dug roots and collected nuts and berries to supplement what charity the primitive community could spare.

Eventually, though, the shame and pain of having contributed to the death of Tsali led Julisdanali to withdraw from even the little society afforded him by this fugitive remnant. He moved further east, away from the soldiers, searching for a secluded place in the Blue Hills that would permit him to live simply and quietly and, he hoped, free from the incessant injustices, wrongs, and sorrows that had crushed his spirit.

He was fighting for his life; not the physical one, where one either succeeds or doesn't, but the emotional one, whose vitality is more difficult to gauge. He hoped to find a place where that part of him that once had found life worth living could be revived. He could not explain why, but he thought that reducing his existence to the basic struggle to survive might be the only hope for the resuscitation of his soul.

And a struggle to survive it was.

In winter his shelter consisted of natural caves or recesses dug into slopes. When it was warmer, he preferred lean-tos fashioned out of sticks and branches or small clearings he made within rhododendron coppices. Fearing discovery, he didn't stay in any one place very long.

The supplies he had when he started out were soon gone. His life depended wholly on what he could eke out of the surroundings. He foraged in the forest. He sometimes brought down a wild turkey or a deer. On occasional forays to the foothills he gleaned from the edges of settler's fields, gathering a little corn and wheat.

These small successes brought him great joy and satisfaction, but the highlight for him was when he tried a trick he had seen used as a boy. First, he crushed some horse chestnuts and ground them into powder. Then he dammed up a stream and released the powder into a pool downstream. Poisoned by the substance, the fish floated to the surface. Julisdanali giddily collected as many as he wanted and then broke the dam. The running water diluted the poison, allowing the groggy, uncaught fish to recover and swim away.

When he went fishing, it was second nature for him to make note of specks of gold in the streambeds or along the banks. He knew this could signify a vein somewhere upstream or uphill. For months he did nothing about these observations but eventually he became so good at survival that he had a little time for recreation. Finding gold fit his definition of a good time, so that is what he set about doing. He wasn't interested in laboring for a few grains, however. He was after the big finds: nuggets, veins, or rich sedimentary deposits.

Fertile fields might forever elude the ungifted, no matter how diligent they were, but the odds of Julisdanali making a significant find were far greater. When he sought out sedimentary gold, he could "see" not only where the stream was, but also where the stream had been in years past. He would envision himself as a particle of gold, being pushed along by the current, swirling in eddies, and finally coming to rest on the bank or on the streambed where the water flowed more slowly, while his less weighty companions continued drifting along. When he found a promising deposit, he would move upstream until the trail petered out, and then he would scour the adjacent slopes for the source of the golden grains.

When he hiked, he rarely missed the green and white-tinged quartz indicative of a place worthy of closer inspection. This was true of many seasoned prospectors, but for most it had taken much trial and error to differentiate false leads from the genuine article. Not so with Julisdanali. Once he had seen the real thing, the characteristics of the rock became ingrained in his consciousness and he no longer concerned himself with time wasting imitations.

So this was how Julisdanali occupied himself; surviving and prospecting, going about each stealthily. To be a Cherokee fugitive was bad enough. To be a trespassing Cherokee fugitive was worse, and there was little land here the takers had not claimed, regardless of how remote or inaccessible. He knew the sentence likely would be executed before he saw a courthouse.

Despite his vigilance, a threat he could not guard against came one winter. A terrible sickness left him so weak that all he could do was lie on his soiled ground mat and stare vacantly through sunken eyes. Near death, he yearned to join his ancestors.

CHAPTER 5
HOMECOMING

THE SUN HAD DROPPED below the hills behind the Gardner home, which made it hard for Aaron to pinpoint the time. As they came within sight of their driveway, he peered through the trees, looking for his father's pickup. He was glad he didn't see it, as this meant they probably weren't late for dinner.

Aaron glanced over his shoulder to check on Kyle; mainly to make sure he wasn't making a move to pass. Aaron's legs felt rubbery, so he was relieved to see that Kyle appeared content with his trailing position. Even better, he appeared to be exhausted, too.

But then, when they were about fifty feet away from their drive, he heard Kyle shout "Race ya!" as he shot past him. The kid was standing on his pedals and cranking like mad.

Aaron had no chance on the bike, but the race continued to the door and his longer stride made the contest a close one. However, Kyle got his hand on the doorknob first.

"Dibs on the bathroom, loser," taunted Kyle as he squirted inside.

Aaron sneered.

The noise the two had made jostling up the steps and across the porch, together with the happy barks of Cheer Boy, their faithful dachshund, heralded their arrival, but Aaron still hollered, "Hi, Mom! We're home!"

"Hi, boys! Dinner's almost ready!"

Walking into the kitchen to join her, Aaron eyed the clock above the sink, and then he called toward the hallway: "Hey, Kyle, we made good time!"

From down the hall, Kyle fired back, "Yeah, but I made better!"

Aaron's lips went "phhttt" in sputtering disregard.

"What was that?" his mom asked, eyeing him questioningly.

"Mouth fart?" he shrugged, and started to fill a glass of water.

He saw her mouth drop open momentarily, then her lips briefly pursed, and then she asked, "How was your adventure?"

Nodding, he replied, "Good," and began to drain the first of what would be several glassfuls of water.

As he stood there gulping, Sandra Gardner hugged him from behind with one of those "where did my little boy go?" hugs. Her sons had reached the age where she about had to be a ninja to get this close.

Uncharacteristically, Aaron didn't protest.

Unwrapping her arms from the damp and malodorous object of her affection, Sandra observed, "My boys have gotten big; hardly boys anymore."

Just then Kyle came into the room and did a surprising thing. He joined them at the sink and wrapped his right arm around his mother's waist. "What's for dinner, Mom?" he asked with his head on her shoulder.

Sandra put her left arm around Kyle and gave him a squeeze. "Miracle meatloaf," she replied happily, "with mashed potatoes, peaches, and, if you behave, frozen chocolate pie with graham cracker crust for dessert."

"Doesn't get any better than that!"

The brothers smiled upon hearing their father's voice.

"Oh, Arthur, I didn't hear you drive up," said Sandra as she walked over to kiss him on the cheek.

"Preoccupied with a couple of good lookin', strappin' young fellers, I suspect," replied Arthur, winking at his sons.

Feigning offense, she whapped him with a dishtowel while the boys stood there grinning.

"I'm famished," he announced, unfazed by his punishment. "Can't wait to dig in to that meatloaf."

"Go on, then, and get washed up," Sandra ordered. "The boys will help set the table."

"Alrighty, I'll go get *warshed*," Arthur replied, taking a poke at Sandra's pronunciation, a product of her Kansas upbringing.

This time, Sandra was not so gentle with the dishtowel.

When Arthur returned (melodramatically rubbing his thigh), they took their places at the table. After Arthur reined in Kyle's premature grazing with a frown, he then offered a prayer.

Although his father's prayers weren't the sort one learns early in life and then mindlessly recites for the rest of it, they did tend to cover certain territory: much thanksgiving, a request for wisdom for their leaders, and a petition for continued blessings. So Aaron didn't feel too guilty about tuning him out and offering a silent prayer of his own covering the same themes: thankfulness (for Lena), wisdom (that he not say anything dumb when he saw her again), and blessings (a buddy with a car so he *could* see her again).

Dinner conversation in the Gardner household usually was deferred until consumption was well underway, and when it got going, it generally didn't stray far from what had happened to each that day and any special happenings in the county. Tonight was no different. Sandra started it off by asking the boys about their hike to the falls.

"What falls?" Arthur interrupted, not having been told of their plans.

Sandra explained that they had ridden their bikes to the trailhead to the waterfall below the youth camp and then hiked down to the falls.

Arthur nodded at his sons' achievement. "Impressive! What route did you take to the trailhead?"

"The shortcut you showed us," answered Aaron.

Arthur just sat there, obviously searching his memory. The longer it took, the more Aaron grinned. Their father had taken them only once, and it was years ago. Too, the route was circuitous and hard to find.

Eventually, and with marked incredulity, came, "Not those old logging roads above Bearwallow Creek?"

Wearing big smiles, Aaron and Kyle nodded.

"Seems my boys are natural pathfinders," commended Arthur, looking impressed. "I didn't think you would be heading that way again; at least without me along. But since you know the way, you need to keep in mind that when you turn off the main road and head toward the ridge you're on property of a hunt club."

Aaron glanced at Kyle and knew they were thinking the same thing: Why must Dad turn every conversation into a lecture?

"This time of year there's probably no need to worry," Arthur continued, "but if you go that way again you should wear hunter orange. And I'd steer clear of the place entirely in the fall or winter."

"So, how *was* your hike?" Sandra again asked.

Before Aaron could answer, Kyle gleefully tattled, "You should have seen Aaron's face when he found a girl in the Ladies' bathroom!"

Aaron instantly protested. "You made it sound like I went in!"

"You would've if the door wasn't locked."

"How was I to know she was in there?"

"What else would've locked herself in there?"

Their voices were getting louder.

"Hold on there, you two," ordered Arthur. "What's all this about?"

Aaron explained about having run out of water while hiking up from the waterfall and their decision to refill their bottles at the chapel.

"*You* decided, not *we*," Kyle corrected.

Ignoring his brother, Aaron went on to tell why he resorted to the women's restroom and why the locked door hadn't clued him in to the fact it was occupied.

"What about that poor girl?" Sandra worried.

Aaron then told them about Lena, concluding with Kyle's offer to take her on a waterfall tour.

"And she really wants to go!" Kyle chimed. "She just loves wattafalls." He finished in a girlie voice and with a flip of the wrist.

Smiling, Arthur asked him, "When are you going and how do you plan to get there?"

Again Kyle didn't hesitate. "We didn't set a day, but she's probably only at camp 'til the end of the week. We hoped you or Mom could drive."

Aaron visibly cringed. Their father could get upset when they failed to get prior clearance before committing either parent.

Not only that, Aaron had hoped to exhaust all other options before asking one of them to chauffeur.

To his surprise, Arthur calmly replied, "Well, do you suppose she would want to make a whole day of it, or were you thinking something shorter?"

Kyle, wearing the look of someone whose plan was going much better than expected, answered, "Probably the whole day, don't you think, Aaron?"

"Yeah, I'd bet so; depending upon what her parents say."

"Understood," Arthur agreed. "Do you have a way to reach her?"

Kyle held up the slip of paper with Lena's phone number.

"Why don't you give her a call to see if Thursday would work? We can take Mom's car and swing down to pick her up before I go to work. I'll drop you kids off at the Raven Cliff Falls trailhead and then come back to get you at lunch. We'll stop for a bite at Sally's Place and then spend the afternoon at the forest. How'd that be?"

"Super!" burst from Kyle, but Aaron was quiet.

"Aaron?"

"No, that'd be great. Thanks Dad."

It had taken Aaron a moment to decide that having a parent drive you is a whole lot better than not going at all.

After dinner was over and the dishwasher was loaded, Arthur, Aaron and Kyle returned to the table and waited for Sandra, who stood at the kitchen counter clearing out the candy wrappers and other trash from Aaron's daypack.

"What's this?" she asked, as much to herself as to anyone.

They turned to see what she was referring to but she was standing with her back toward them.

"Lacking x-ray vision, we're going to have a bit of trouble weighing in on that one," muttered Arthur as he continued to shuffle a deck of playing cards.

Aaron watched her lean forward, as if she was studying something intently. Then she spoke, the words coming out slowly, like they would from someone just learning to read.

The three at the table reacted as if they had just been goosed, obviously astonished that this innocent, sweet woman had said such a thing.

Apparently, it shocked her too. When she turned to face them, she looked mortified.

"Sandra Jean Gardner, did you just say, 'That bastard'?"

Looking at Arthur like a puppy that had just piddled where it oughtn't, Sandra shook her head in inconsistent denial. Still mute, she brought the file over to the table and handed it to him, wordlessly urging him to read it for himself.

"Made in U.S.A." he announced, eyeing her quizzically.

With a huff, she grabbed the tip of the tool and flipped it over.

When the small upper case letters came into focus, Arthur firmly announced his findings in a monotone voice: "FLAT BASTARD."

Sandra straightened up, looking vindicated. The brothers traded guilty smiles and tried not to laugh. Arthur, wearing a little grin, sat there quietly for a moment, surveying the others, before delivering his tutorial.

"This is a steel file," he began, stating the obvious. "This particular kind is known as a bastard."

As she took a seat opposite from Arthur, Sandra shot her sons a stern "listen to your father" glare, cutting off their titters.

"Now, I'm no expert on files," Arthur continued, "but I know there are at least two kinds of bastards...."

At this, Kyle put his hand over his mouth to restrain a laugh but it came out through his nose as a snort, along with some snot. Aaron strived to contain himself, too. He dropped his head, pursed his lips and clasped his belly to stop it from jiggling. He sounded remarkably like a hyena.

Even their mother giggled.

Arthur did not stop. "There are round bastards, which, of course, are round, and then there are flat bastards, like this one; flat-sided."

The deadpan delivery of this factual statement allowed the brothers to get themselves under control. Teary-eyed Aaron nodded to signal his understanding and Kyle grabbed a paper napkin and wiped his nose.

Arthur began to twist the file back and forth in front of his eyes. "Just what makes a bastard a bastard, I'm not sure," he continued, "but I know one when I see one."

Sandra gasped. Aaron, ordinarily averse to encouraging his father's dry wit, openly granted him kudos by laughing freely. This time, it was Kyle who was reduced to tears.

Arthur now joined in the merriment.

"Boys," Sandra uttered with a slow shake of her head to demonstrate her disdain for their brutish ways. However, she was unable to keep a smile off her face; her pretense delighting her three heathen all the more.

After order was restored, Arthur asked his sons how they came to have the file and Aaron gave an account of its discovery.

"Why do you think it was there, Dad?" Kyle asked.

"I haven't the foggiest," he confessed, handing the file to Aaron, "but if Thursday's going to work out for your waterfall tour, why don't you bring this thing long? We can go find Charlie and see what he thinks."

The brothers' faces lit up at their father's suggestion.

Charles Barnes—"Charlie" to his acquaintances—was the bulldozer operator at the state forest. He was an interesting fellow who seemed to know something about everything. Although he was old enough to retire had he wanted to, somehow he was able to relate so well to the Gardner brothers that they considered him one of their closest friends.

Arthur picked up the deck of cards and scooted his chair closer to the table. He eyed his sons in turn. "Alright, you novices ready for a lesson?" he challenged, and tamped the deck on edge.

CHAPTER 6
PASSING THE BUCK

AARON'S PALMS were sweating. It felt like an electrical current was coursing through him. To quell his anxiety he began to inwardly chant a portion of a Bible verse he had memorized: *Be anxious for nothing…Be anxious for nothing…Be anxious for nothing.*

After a few rounds of cards Aaron had asked Kyle for Lena's number and then had taken the phone into his bedroom so he could have some privacy. But he knew he needed to calm down before he made the call. Telling himself not to be anxious didn't seem to be working, though. *Maybe some other Scripture.* He remembered the story of Joshua; how when he was on the verge of leading the Israelites into the Promised Land, God had repeatedly admonished him to be strong and courageous. So Aaron recited the command like a mantra, hoping to internalize the words and somehow make them work for him, too.

He grew calm, but when he moved his index finger toward the phone both of his hands began to tremble. "Sh…oot," he muttered.

Didn't Shakespeare write something about screwing one's courage to the sticking place? He chewed on this for a bit. *How does one go about screwing it in? How do you know when it is stuck?* No answers came.

He had been here almost fifteen minutes. If he was going to act, he had to do it soon. Lena might be heading to bed or, worse, Kyle might come to look for him. He pounded his leg and through gritted teeth growled, "Just do it."

Resting his forearm against the desk to keep the phone still, he carefully entered each number.

He listened as the ring tones began to sound their refrain. Unfortunately, he could also hear Kyle calling for him and his voice was getting louder. Aaron's neck muscles grew taut and his lips contorted into a horizontal figure eight, clenched molars visible at both ends.

He turned toward the door, fearing Kyle would burst through any second. Distracted, he didn't hear Lena's father answer the phone.

All Grady Summerlin heard was deep breathing. "Pervert," he said disgustedly, and ended the call.

Aaron was aghast.

Suddenly, Kyle popped in and shouted down the hall, "He's still in the bedroom talking to his girlfriend!"

Aaron, mouth agape, rallied enough to mount a rebuttal, "She's not my girlfriend...and...and I'm not talking to her!"

"Turned you down, huh?"

I'm gonna kill him. "No," Aaron replied as calmly as he was able, "I didn't get through to her."

"Let me try."

Aaron's immediate impulse was to reject the offer, but then realized that it might afford him a way out of his predicament. *When Mr. Summerlin answers, Kyle can deny having just called. And he won't come across as some blithering idiot.* Aaron handed him the phone and Lena's number.

Kyle made the call.

"Who is this?" barked an angry voice from the little speaker. Aaron didn't need the phone by his ear to hear it.

"Kuh...kuh...Kyle Gardner?" came his brother's stuttering and uncertain reply.

Aaron knew where the conversation was headed and he was feeling really smug. He put his ear next to Kyle's.

"Did you just call here?" the man demanded to know.

"Uh, no, that was my brother Aaron."

Aaron's chin dropped to his chest and his hands flew up to clasp his head. Alas, the cat was out of the bag, the milk was spilt, the end had come. Dazed and despairing, he slowly walked out of the bedroom, down the hall, through the living room, past his parents' concerned and watchful eyes, and out the front door. Cheer Boy trailed at his heels.

CHAPTER 7
THE BUCK STOPS HERE

MEANWHILE, MR. SUMMERLIN asked Kyle why his brother hadn't said anything. Kyle confided that Aaron had called to speak to Lena but since he was afraid of girls he might have been unable to talk. Sensing an opening, Kyle asked if Lena was there.

"Yeah, but keep it short," the man replied gruffly.

"Aaron?"

"No, it's Kyle," he replied, surprised at how quickly Lena came to the phone.

"Oh, hi Kyle! Daddy said it was a boy and I just assumed it was Aaron."

"He tried, but he…uh…umm…he had some technical difficulties," he offered, uncharacteristically protective of his brother's dignity.

"Oh," she said quietly, and then added, "Did you get home all right?"

"Yep, no problems; and guess what?" Kyle went on to tell her the waterfall tour was a go and summarized the proposed itinerary. He could tell she was excited, asking him to "wait a little minute" while she asked permission.

Soon, an adult version of the same lovely accent came through the earpiece.

"Hello Kyle, this is Lena's mother speaking. Is your mother there? I'd like to visit with her briefly, if I may."

"Sure, Mrs.…uh…Lena's mom…just a minute." Kyle felt stupid for having come up blank when he tried to think of Lena's last name.

Kyle hustled into the living room and told his mother that Lena's mom wanted to speak with her. Sandra took it from there. It wasn't long before she had her feet drawn up on the couch, chatting on the phone as if she and Mrs. Summerlin were dearest friends.

Wondering whether the call would ever end, Kyle was about to leave the room when Sandra looked up at him with a smile and nod.

Kyle immediately turned to Arthur. "Dad! Do you know where….?"

Before Kyle finished the question, Arthur looked up from the newspaper and nodded toward the porch.

Kyle ran out and found Aaron sitting on the front steps with a hand on Cheer Boy's head, looking into the night.

"Hey, Lena can go!"

CHAPTER 8
SADIE'S INHERITANCE

Back to Atlanta,
A few hours after the attic episode

SITTING ALONE at a corner table in his regular hangout, he was consoling himself over a few drinks. His "expert", a drinking buddy who dealt in goods having ownership "issues", had bluntly informed him that his choice antiques were junk; he'd be lucky to get a hundred bucks from the entire lot.

Remembering the envelope, he pulled it out of his pocket and removed the contents. He carefully unfolded the papers to find a long letter and a hand-drawn map. He started with the letter.

July 26, 1854

Dearest Sadie,

It is difficult to know how to tell you this, so I will just put it plain. I am your brother James. You must have thought you were forgotten or that I had died. I cannot explain why I did not write. Perhaps I thought it best if you were to forget your first family and become a Williams in heart as well as name. I pray you will forgive me and that this letter will not cause you grief. The doctor says the days left to me are not many and it seems good to me that you should know these truths.

You must know the only reason our mother did not take you with her on the trail where our people cried was because she feared you would not survive. She cared for you dearly. If perchance you have had word of her, would you kindly write to me posthaste? It would quiet my dreams to know she arrived safely and fared well in the west.

As for me, I hid in the hills where I could live away from the takers and not be made to leave the land of our ancestors. Many days I did not know whether I would see another sunrise. It was during one of these dark times that Mr. Tucker happened upon my camp. I was near death. With no little hardship to himself, he tended me like a babe until my health returned. With his help and companionship, I have been content these many years.

The lawyer we hired to find you wrote that you found a good man and provided me with a niece who is nearing the age you were when I last saw you. Glory be! It is a might hard to imagine little Sadie a wife and mother. I am most sorry I was not a better uncle for your child, but perhaps I can make your lives easier.

Do you recall when our father sent me to work in the mines? Turns out prospecting suited my fancy, though I never had much use for the yellow stuff. Some years back I found a promising vein and had begun to work it when a passel of trouble soured me on the endeavor. I closed the hole and turned to hunting ginseng instead. This kept me in tobacco and other necessaries without the worry.

Mr. Tucker and I shan't have any need of gold in the time left to us and he has no relatives he cares to remember so we agreed you should have it. We have drawnt you a map to show the way. Be assured the little mine holds great promise, but is a might hard to reach. I still recall the day I shinny down the rope and dig like a badger into what looks like a nest of yellow jackets. A heap of shiners, I tell you. I stuff my pockets and up I go.

We posted the ore to Milledgeville in two batches, believing it safer than shipping it to the U. S. Mint in Philadelphia, but we were mistaken. Soon after receiving the coins minted from the first batch, we learnt that scalawags robbed our second one. Then merchants tell us our pretty coins were short of gold and twarnt legal tender. It was then I decided to seal up the hole. I put those worthless coins in there too, wanting to be done with them, but they will still have value if you melt them down.

Do you remember how we stole out one night to watch our people do the booger dance around the fire? I had told Mr. Tucker about the masked dancers, so he molds a cast of my face and uses it to fashion a clay plate that served nicely to plug that hole. He cooked it for many an hour in a fiery pit, so it is blackened and not easy to spy. The feller who comes to fetch the gold best be holding fast onto that rope when he climbs down to see Julisdanali staring back at him. I'd wager there will be another waterfall along the clift that day.

Keep aholt of your tongue for word of gold brings out the skunks. And do not try to get at the hole from below. I tried it when I was tracking that vein and learnt my lesson then. A body coming at it thataways is apt to end up in pieces at the foot of the clift.

I am sending you another present. Mr. Tucker made the jug hisself. I fear you will think its visage awful but it testifies to his skills, for it is a fair likeness. Look upon it and know you are seeing the face of one who has always cared for you.

I must close as I am as worn out as an old shoe. I have not written this much since old buzzard Jenkins made me copy Apostle Paul's letter to the Ephesians after he caught me smoking behind the mission school.

Mr. Tucker says you must stop by for a visit if you travel to these parts. Most anyone around here can direct you to the cabin. It is less than a day's journey from the mine. Would that I could greet you but unless you fly like the hawk, I fear it is not to be.

With utmost affection,
James Julisdanali Streeter

At first he wasn't much interested in the old letter; some chicken fingers were getting most of his attention. But with the writer's mention of gold, the remainder of the greasy sticks sat untouched. After reading and re-reading the letter, he turned his attention to the map. It clearly showed the intersection of the states of Georgia and the Carolinas, plus a few place names he recognized. The amateur cartographer had drawn an inset focusing in on one area, so he examined it more closely. Situated along a "clift" near a waterfall on what might be a "Rooster" or "Booster" "Crick," or "Creek" was an oval shape with eyes and mouth. This, he was sure, marked the mine's location.

The lure of the precious metal was strong. It drew him in as it had thousands before him. The slightest chance the gold was still there was reason enough to put his best efforts into finding the mine, he decided. He started a mental checklist of things he needed to do.

When he caught himself worrying about how he was going to turn the raw gold into dollars, he knew he needed to slow down and take things one step at a time. *If the gold is still there after all this time, surely it will stay put a while longer.*

CHAPTER 9
OFF TO CAMP

First day of Family Camp
A few days before the file was found

LOCATING AN IDEAL place to base the search had taken him less than a week. He discovered a camp, complete with cabins and a dining hall, situated directly north of the cliff. But there was one problem: it was a *youth* camp, and he was sure they weren't about to accept a middle-aged man as one of their registrants.

Several minutes of bouncing around the camp's website and he had the solution. One week each summer was set aside for families.

Hardly a candidate for father of the year and certainly no outdoorsman, it had flabbergasted his wife and daughter when he suggested they attend. But after listening to his sales pitch and checking out the website, they agreed to the trip.

The Saturday marking the beginning of the weeklong camp finally had arrived. Now he would find out whether his months of preparation would pay off. He was both anxious and excited.

Though not a morning person, he had insisted on a 6 a.m. departure. For him, getting ready was usually a last minute scramble, but he had packed the car the night before. Still, it irked him that his wife kept looking at him like he was some stranger.

The trip to camp was beautiful and uneventful. His wife and daughter entertained each other while he did the driving, his mind half on the road and half on planning what he would do after they arrived.

Tucked into the hazy, forested Blue Hills, just north of the South Carolina border, the camp was miles off the highway, down a winding road leading away from civilization. As he pulled up to the administration building at the entrance, his wife complimented him on what little difficulty he had finding the place. He didn't tell her that he had been there once before.

Less than two weeks earlier he had taken a sick day at work and made a clandestine foray, hoping to get a look at the cliff and find the waterfall depicted on the old map. By day's end he had accomplished neither, but he did manage to find a promising trail and get his climbing gear stashed in a rhododendron thicket.

I'll do better today, he assured himself.

No sooner had they checked in and got their things transferred into the cabin before he jettisoned his wife and daughter and set off to find the trail he had seen on his earlier visit.

He looked fairly well prepared for a short hike. A baseball cap shaded his head. A pair of binoculars hung from his neck. A bottle of water and a small flashlight were attached to his belt. His pockets bulged with supplies of one sort or another. For footwear he had chosen jogging shoes.

When he came to the road skirting the camp he should have turned left but went right and didn't realize his mistake until he saw the dining hall up ahead. He knew it was west of where he wanted to be. Although he didn't have to backtrack far, it worried him to know how easy it was to get lost in these woods.

The humidity was oppressive. He was dripping with sweat when he reached the trailhead. His solid colored ball cap appeared two-toned. Nevertheless, he strode energetically down the trail.

He spent the next half hour dodging tree roots, ankle-twisting-sized rocks and shirt snagging vegetation but he had yet to find a place giving him a good view of the cliff. Worse, he was out of water. His vigor and optimism had waned. He was tempted to turn back, but then he reflected upon the prize that awaited him.

The trail became steeper. In places it crossed slabs of fallen rock and passed over, between, or around boulders. Occasionally he feared he had lost the trail. He constantly had to watch his feet.

Coming to the top of a rocky outcropping, he worried that he had taken a wrong turn, but then he saw a rope hanging over the edge. He clambered over the side, skinning a knuckle in the process.

The going got harder. He occasionally had to carefully pick his way through piles of jagged rocks. Sometimes the trail was so steep that his feet would slide out from under him.

Eventually, it became clear he was dropping into a canyon. This had been a big mistake; the trail had veered away from the cliff. Where it led he didn't know, but he wasn't going to go to the trouble of finding out.

Back up the trail he went, sometimes pulling himself forward using tree roots or branches. His head and heart were pounding. He was cotton-mouthed. His forehead was dry and hot. He kept his eyes on the ground as this somehow seemed to make it easier. Progress was slow.

When he came to the rope, he stopped and stared at the wall in front of him. Then he whimpered, crossed his hands in front of his face and leaned against the huge rock with his forehead on his forearm. The ledge was only a few feet above his head, but dehydration and the insufferable heat and humidity had done him in.

He stood there a couple of minutes, then ran his dry tongue over a bead of slimy crud on his upper lip, grasped the rope and began to climb. At the top, he leaned over the ledge and supported himself with his arms, locking his elbows beneath him. Next, he pivoted on the heel of his right hand while drawing up his right thigh in an attempt to bring his seat to rest on the lip. Had his energy not already been spent, it may have worked, but his bulging cargo pocket slowed his pivot and he came down on the side of his leg, with the rock edge jamming up the pocket's contents.

The rock's edge became a fulcrum. Fearing the scale would tip in favor of his lower body and cause him to slide off, he leaned sideways over the path as far as he could. This brought his fatty spare tire into painful contact with something sharp and hard. Afraid to move lest he fall off the rock and considering what to do next, he let the object jab him awhile.

Then, with his locked arms holding him in place, he gingerly rotated back to his starting position, leaned forward as far as he could, and made like a walrus; pulling and pushing his body forward while dragging his belly through the dust until he could get to his knees. To be safe, he crawled up the path a couple of yards before struggling to his feet.

He lifted his shirt to inspect the damage and saw a diagonal abrasion. Three small but distinct creases came together at a bright red dot at the upper end. He touched the tender spot and then stared at his hand. *Blood.* He looked down at his cargo pocket, all bunched up from its service as a brake. His steel file, pointy end up, was sticking out the top.

Angry with himself for having brought the useless thing and cursing the hardware store for selling it without a handle, he pulled out the file and flung it hard.

He stayed there for a time, bent over with his hands on his thighs, until his breathing returned to normal. Then he surveyed his surroundings.

Before, he had been intent on only one thing; getting a good look at the cliff face. But, oddly, now he noticed the various colors and shapes of the rocks and vegetation. He found the contrasts interesting. Except for the pain from his scraped side and his dry mouth, he liked the way he felt. Somehow his head seemed less cluttered; less compressed. Some water would be nice, but he knew he could make it back without any. He wasn't afraid. For the first time in his adult life he began to think of hiking as something to do just for fun.

Resuming his upward trek, he soon came to a place where the trail crossed a slanted rock slab covered by loose gravel. On the way down he had stayed low and kept to the edge but going up it didn't seem as treacherous, so he walked erect. This allowed him to catch a glimpse of a chalky wall off to his right.

He stopped and tried to get a better look. He found that he still could not see much, but from the lack of any visible intervening ridge he guessed the cliff stretched a considerable distance in his direction.

Once again the clay face monopolized his thoughts. Eagerly anticipating tomorrow's search, he hustled up the trail.

CHAPTER 10
TOIL AND TROUBLE

NIGHT HAD FALLEN on his fourth day at camp and he had yet to see any sign of the mine. He hadn't even found the waterfall. Lying in bed, unable to sleep, he was bummed.

After wasting Saturday on the trail to who-knows-where, he had spent the better part of each ensuing day exploring the cliff face. This entailed rappelling down several feet, sidestepping in both directions, and then repeating the process as many times as it took to know the mine wasn't in that vertical slice of the cliff. He would then laboriously ascend to the top, move his equipment west, re-anchor his ropes, and do it all over again. He felt like a slow motion yo-yo.

To maintain the appearance that he was just a happy camper, he would occasionally interrupt the process and return to camp to halfheartedly participate in some scheduled family activity. He worried he would have to do this for the duration. His body ached. His feet were sore. His head hurt. The constant back and forth was wearing him out.

Making matters worse, tomorrow he was supposed to go to the camp's ropes course. He didn't like to think about all the time and energy that was apt to take. He began to think that attending family camp as a cover hadn't been such a good idea. In fact, he was questioning the whole endeavor.

He blamed his wife and daughter. It was because of them he was attending so many camp activities, yet apparently it wasn't enough. Last night, his wife had chewed him out for spending so little time with their daughter. She said it was worse than if they had stayed at home; at least there she wouldn't have expected much from him; he was hardly ever there. Oh, the look she had given him.

He wanted to defend himself; tell her that at least he was doing something constructive; not spending every night in the bar like he used to. But he was afraid he might say something that would give away his true purpose. Sharing the wealth might be okay if there was a boatload of it, but if not? Well, he'd rather keep the fruits of his labors to himself. So he bit his tongue and merely said that he would try to do better.

Instead of being pissed, she ought to be impressed at what I've done; at all the work I've put in. Man, if she knew. He reflected on all his preparations; all the expense and trouble. He had read how-to books about mountaineering until his eyes glazed over. He had trained so much on his health club's indoor climbing wall that his thighs no longer fit in some of his pants. He had frequented a tree climbing school in suburban Atlanta until he could use ascenders to climb vertical rope faster than some of the veteran arborists in attendance.

He had not neglected mineralogy, either. He had wrestled with books and articles he never before would have touched. He drove to Dahlonega, a town about sixty miles northeast of Atlanta, to visit its Gold Museum after being told about it by a reference desk librarian (until the librarian clued him in, he hadn't even known that Georgia had a gold rush).

It had been the museum's docent, an arthritic old rock hound, who taught him what a mineral identification field kit should contain and gave him instructions on how to use the various tools. The docent also recommended a gem and mineral club in Atlanta, which provided him valuable hands-on experience. It still amazed him that one of the club members raided his own supplies to provide him with hard-to-find items for his field kit.

Then he relaxed and stopped trying to itemize all he had learned; all he had done. Somehow, the memory of the interesting, strangely generous folks he had met along the way had quieted his mind.

He began to listen to the night sounds.

Soon, he slept.

CHAPTER 11
PICKING UP A GIRL

AARON AWOKE to the sounds of someone rustling around in the kitchen. He had set the alarm, but it had yet to buzz. Any other day he might have waited for it to go off, but he hopped out of bed and went over to wake Kyle. However, when he saw his brother's peaceful face, he let him sleep.

Aaron found Arthur standing at the kitchen counter waiting for the coffeemaker to wring the last dribbles from its innards. The aroma made such an early rising bearable, Aaron reckoned.

His dad shot him a grin. "Wanna cup?"

The offer took Aaron by surprise. For years his father had warned that the beverage would stunt his growth and make his hair curly.

"Sure!"

Arthur set a steaming cup in front of him.

Aaron felt a bit nervous. He wasn't sure whether it was because his dad was watching him or because the drink was so hot. Cautiously, he took a sip.

Aaron swallowed, and then turned up his nose.

Arthur smiled. "Too bad the taste doesn't match the smell, huh?"

Without altering his expression, Aaron nodded.

"Don't give up; there is such a thing as a good cup of coffee. I just haven't stumbled upon the right formula yet. Sometime when we're in town I'll buy you a cup of the good stuff."

Arthur moved over to the stove and lifted the lid of a pot to check on his handiwork. "Looks about ready. Better go get your brother," he directed. He had prepared the oatmeal the old fashioned way, on the stove, using milk, and with raisins, dried cranberries and walnuts stirred in for good measure.

Except for an occasional Saturday, breakfast in the Gardner household was ordinarily an "every man for himself" affair. *Dad must be treating this day special, too,* Aaron thought, as he turned to go, but before he took two steps, his pajama-clad sibling shuffled in.

Kyle moved zombie-like to the kitchen table and took his seat, as if he expected someone to wait upon him—which they did. Aaron poured the juice and put bread in the toaster while Arthur dished up the oatmeal and brought it to the table.

Staring fixedly at the tabletop with half-opened eyes and seemingly oblivious to the bowl of oatmeal in front of him, Kyle anticipated the exact spot where Aaron was going to set the juice glass, grasped it before it touched down and swept it to his lips like an assembly line robot. After chugging it, he returned to his head-down position, picked up a spoon without looking, and rhythmically devoured the oatmeal. Ignoring the toast, the automaton then rose to his feet and shuffled back down the hallway, leaving the others to wonder whether he was heading to the shower or returning to bed.

A few minutes later Sandra came in. Arthur alerted her to the hot oatmeal on the stove, but instead of getting a bowl she asked the two about that day's itinerary and about what the hikers were taking to eat. Then she opened the cupboard. "I'll put together some extra snacks for you, just in case," she announced.

After thanking his dad for the breakfast and his mom for the goodies, Aaron returned to the bedroom. He had checked his day pack the previous evening to make sure it held the usual supplies: water bottle, first aid kit, toilet paper, trowel, bug repellent, knife, compass, whistle, emergency blanket, lightweight poncho and trail mix, plus a water bottle and poncho for Lena in case she needed them. He had made sure Kyle assembled his gear, too, so aside from brushing his teeth and filling his water bottle there wasn't much left for him to do. However, Aaron was glad to have a little solitude; he was getting a little jittery and was afraid it might show through his face.

At the appointed time, the brothers assembled at their mother's car, packs in hand. Thinking ahead to the rendezvous with Lena, Aaron was quick to get in the back seat, allowing Kyle to sit up front. Sandra stood on the porch and waved goodbye as Arthur backed out of the drive.

"Oh that bastard!" Arthur growled.

The brothers' heads popped up. Never had they heard their dad speak this way about anyone.

Arthur looked over his shoulder at Aaron and calmly asked, "Did you bring it?"

Oh, THAT bastard, Aaron realized.

"Yep," Aaron replied. "It's in my pack."

It dawned on him that his dad may have planned this just to see their reaction. Aaron looked into the rear view mirror and grinned. Reflected there were his dad's smiling eyes; deep creases spreading from their corners like rays of the sun.

To get to the camp, Arthur took the same roller coaster route he drove to work. The road carried them across a mountain valley and then up a fairly steep grade until topping out near the crest of the range, where they began to wind and undulate through the mountains.

The motion apparently lulled Kyle asleep—his head, with mouth agape and eyes shut, was propped against the car door. But about ten minutes after passing the entrance to the state forest they went around a sharp curve, momentarily jarring him awake. "Where are we?" he mumbled.

"Won't be long before we hit the turn-off to the camp," Arthur replied.

From the looks of him, Kyle already had gone back to sleep, but Aaron shifted to where he could check his hair in the rear view mirror.

Soon, Arthur braked to a stop where the road teed into the highway running south from Brevard. "Time to wake up, sunshine," he said, pinching Kyle in the ribs.

Kyle stirred, but his eyes remained closed. After making the turn, Arthur pinched him again, harder.

Kyle stretched and then massaged his neck. "Time?" he asked amidst a yawn.

"Just after 7:15," Arthur answered. "It's taking us a little longer than I thought."

Every inch of the route was scenic, but Aaron liked this portion best. Huge old pines and hemlocks crowded the highway, giving it the look of a path through an enchanted forest.

The turn-off to camp lay nearly concealed behind a wooded hillside ahead on their left. Equipped with a local's navigational advantage, Arthur made the turn, leaving them a drive of only five miles or so.

They were now traveling east along the rim of the escarpment delineating the border between the states. These highlands were in North Carolina. South Carolina was in the low country to their right. In places, the difference in elevation was almost two thousand feet.

An opening through the trees would occasionally afford them a view of the foothills—small mountains, really. The sun had cleared the tops of the mounds, but the haze was still thick in the valleys, giving it the look of piles and piles of billowy, blue pillows.

A few more dips in the road and they were at the camp. The only car in the small lot in front of the cabin-sized administration building was a mid-sized sedan with a Georgia license plate. Arthur parked beside it. No one was inside.

Aaron heard the sound of moving water. Through the windows of the adjacent car he saw a small waterfall. Then he noticed movement off to one side of the administration building. An attractive middle-aged woman and a girl were walking toward them.

Arthur got out, and then poked his head back in. "Come on guys," he ordered.

Once out of the car, Aaron could see that the waterfall was actually the spillway of a small lake with a beach and waterslide. His main focus, though, was on the approaching pair or, to be more exact, on the younger of them.

With a big wave, Lena called out excitedly, "Hey, Aaron! Hey, Kyle!"

"Hey Lena!" shouted Kyle.

Aaron just gulped, shielding himself with the open car door.

"Mr. Gardner?" said the woman as she extended her hand. "I'm Lena's mother, Linda Summerlin."

She talks just like Lena, thought Aaron.

With a smile and nod, Arthur returned the handshake. "Call me Arthur. And here are my two, uh, associates; Dan'l Boone and Davy Crockett."

Aaron reddened.

Mrs. Summerlin greeted the brothers by their correct names.

Arthur asked her if they were enjoying their stay.

"It's certainly a beautiful place," she replied somewhat vaguely, and quickly addressed her daughter. "Lena, best get your pack. We don't want to make Mr. Gardner late."

Lena was a step ahead of her, having already retrieved the pack and handed it to Aaron. Aaron raised the pack in the air to show Mrs. Summerlin he had it.

"Okay, guys, looks like we're set. Why don't you two sit in the back and let our guest ride up front," suggested Arthur.

Aagh, torpedoed by my own dad, thought Aaron.

Arthur turned to Mrs. Summerlin. "The plan is to get Lena back here around six this evening. Will that work all right?"

"That will be perfect," she replied, "They serve until 6:30, so if you could drop her off by the dinin' hall, she can join us for dinner."

"Will do. See you then."

Mrs. Summerlin leaned through the passenger door's open window and gave Lena a peck on the cheek. "Have a good time, dear, and be careful."

"I will, Mom. You have a good time, too. Tell Daddy bye, if you see him."

On their way back to the highway, they were as animated as a family leaving on vacation. The Gardners paid rapt attention as Lena told about the camp. When she talked about canoeing and again when she described the ropes course, Kyle bemoaned the fact that they weren't attending camp, too.

Aaron thought it odd that Lena had mentioned her mother participating in some of the camp activities, but had said nothing of her father.

He was not the only one to notice. As they turned onto the highway, Kyle blurted, "What's your dad been doing?"

When she didn't answer right away, Arthur looked over at her, but instead of repeating Kyle's question, he asked her what she had packed for the hike.

Aaron was sure that his dad had intentionally changed the subject, and he was fairly sure that he knew why: something about her father was bothering her; something heavy.

However, Lena showed no sign of being under any cloud when she gave Arthur an accounting of the contents of her pack.

"Impressive," he commended.

"You forgot the TP," critiqued Kyle.

Lena gasped and swiveled in her seat. "Y'all don't think we might get stranded for the night, do you?"

"You mean the urge hasn't ever hit you all the sudden?" Kyle asked incredulously.

While his dad chuckled, Aaron intervened. "Wait a minute. You two aren't talking the same language." He turned to Kyle. "She thinks you meant a teepee; you know, an Indian tent."

Lena nodded.

This time it was Kyle who turned red, a rare occurrence. He forced out an, "Oh."

Arthur inclined his head toward Lena. "For a long hike, it's a good idea to stuff the squashed tail end of a roll of toilet paper in a plastic bag, together with a little plastic shovel and a few packages of hand wipes like you sometimes get at barbeque or fried chicken joints."

With that trail tidbit, Arthur brought the car to a rolling stop at the trailhead to Raven Cliff Falls.

CHAPTER 12
FAST FRIENDS

THE TRIO STOPPED at the trailhead marker to fill out the hiker registration forms. While Aaron took care of the paperwork, Kyle sampled some walking sticks left by previous hikers.

"Here, Lena, do you want one of these?" he asked, holding out one of the sticks.

"Thank you, Kyle."

Hearing that voice made Aaron wish he had been the one to ask.

The trail was well maintained and gentle enough that a walking stick really wasn't needed, but hiking with one in hand seemed like the right thing to do, so the brothers each grabbed one too. Thus equipped, they marched down the wide trail, their legs and sticks swinging in unison. It made a fine picture; the morning light filtering through the trees to paint leafy shadows on their contented backs.

At the bottom of the long incline, the trail narrowed to where only two could walk abreast. Since Lena was answering Kyle's questions about the camp's ropes course, Aaron dropped back, shoulders drooping. After taking his trailing position, he overheard only snippets of Lena's answers, but he did note a marked shift in her tone; chipper at the beginning and quieter at the end. He could not tell whether she grew sad at the telling or simply became winded from the steady climb.

Before long, they came to a place where the one trail became three. A trailhead marker at this junction showed that the upper and lower trails actually were the same trail, comprising a loop which circuited the top of the falls. The middle trail led to the Raven Cliff Falls overlook, and this was the one they took.

They had just started down this trail when Kyle dispassionately announced, "Snake," tapping his walking stick ahead of him, toward his left.

It was not unusual to encounter snakes while hiking the trails. They liked to warm themselves in the sun; especially during the cooler parts of the day. Most would slither away once they felt the vibrations of man's approach, but sometimes a stubborn or sleepy one would hold its ground. This was not one of those confrontational occasions, however. Its front half already had disappeared into the grass at the edge of the trail before Kyle spotted the creature.

At the word "snake" Lena grasped Aaron's right arm with both hands and pulled him to her. He didn't know whether she was trying to pull him out of harm's way or use him as a shield. Either way, he wasn't complaining.

"He's gone," advised Kyle. "Didja see him?"

"Just caught the tail end," answered Aaron, patting Lena reassuringly.

"Are ya' sure it's gone?" she shuddered.

"Yep, long gone," assured Kyle, turning his head in their direction.

The look of disapproval that washed over Kyle's face couldn't be missed. Aaron and Lena moved apart.

Silence reigned for a time, which was just as well because the trail began to climb unrelentingly, taxing even these young sets of lungs.

After about twenty minutes of this slog, Aaron noticed that the canopy had begun to thin; the trail was now carpeted in mottled patches of sunlight. He looked up and saw open sky through the trees straight ahead. It signaled to him that they were almost at their destination.

"Kyle, why don't you let Lena take the lead?"

Somewhat remarkably, Kyle obliged.

Lena had not been in front long when the trail dropped sharply to their left and opened onto a small clearing along the mountainside. She stopped at the top of the clearing, her eyes raised toward the mountain opposite from the one on which they stood. Big, dark birds soared and circled above its flanks.

On his first visit, Aaron had paused there, too, wondering why that mountain seemed different from the others; darker, more mysterious. He had decided it was the trees. The mountains around here were blanketed by leafy, deciduous trees, but not that one. It was covered mostly by dark evergreens— hemlocks, he guessed.

Seeing the birds again made him question his hypothesis. He could not recall a time when he had *not* seen them there and, as before, they flew like airborne sentries: always circling, seldom crossing over into the airspace above the neighboring hills, and quickly returning when they did.

What is it about that place?

His imaginings were cut short when Lena dropped down into the clearing. He didn't want to miss seeing her reaction when she saw what brought them here. He hustled to catch up.

A simple, backless bench sat at the far side of the clearing. As Lena drew near it, she gasped and froze in place.

In the distance, rising unexpectedly from the cleavage dividing the two mountains, was a massive black wall: Raven Cliff. And from this high vantage point, one could see not only the spectacular waterfall which poured over it, but also the river which fed the waterfall; a lively thing that cascaded and stair-stepped down through the lushly forested mountainside.

The brothers drew close; flanking her, saying nothing. Aaron turned and looked at Lena's face in profile. A drop formed at the corner of her eye and then slid down her cheek in a glistening line.

"So beautiful," she said softly, echoing his thoughts.

After a few moments, Aaron unshouldered his pack and took a seat on the bench, facing Raven Cliff. "Anybody hungry?" he asked, throwing open the flap. Plopping down on either side of him, his companions took a look at what the pack had to offer.

Lena looked at Aaron. "Why'd y'all bring a file?"

"It's a real bastard!" Kyle interjected.

Aaron shot Kyle a perturbed glance and then turned back to Lena, who now looked bewildered.

"Bastard is the name for the kind of file it is," Aaron explained. "We found it on our hike to the waterfall the day we met you and we brought it along to see if one of Dad's co-workers might have an idea of what it was doing down there."

Kyle stopped chewing on a piece of beef jerky long enough to add, "Charlie knows something about everything."

"My father has one like it," Lena observed.

"That right?" said Aaron, without much interest.

Lena nodded, adding, "He got it at the hardware store last week when we went to get some supplies for the trip."

"Hmm." Having stuffed two orange slices in his mouth, it was all Aaron could manage.

Before long, the sun shone directly on them and it grew unpleasantly warm. Lena seemed content to sit and admire the scenery, though, so Aaron suffered in silence. From the way Kyle was squirming, he guessed he felt the same.

Kyle was the first to speak. "Let's head back," he demanded. "I'm roasting!"

"Me, too!" said Lena, popping up off the bench.

Kyle's head spun toward her. "Why didn't you say something? We've been waiting on you!"

"Ah…I'm sorry. I didn't want to hurry y'all." The hurt in her voice was as plain as the irritation was in his.

They hadn't traveled far when Aaron noticed a flame azalea in full bloom near the trail. He detoured to pluck one of its yellow-orange clusters while Kyle and Lena continued on in silence. Catching up, Aaron offered Lena his version of an olive branch.

"Why thank you, Aaron. They're so pretty." Her voice hinted that the cloud had passed.

Soon, they came to a long and straight downhill grade. "Who's the fastest skipper?" Lena demanded to know as she cast aside her walking stick.

Although "skipper" sounded like "skippa," the challenge was plain enough, and Kyle was after her in a flash. Aaron hesitated, not having skipped in years, and feeling it a tad childish, but after watching Kyle he decided he could do no worse, so he joined in, too.

Early in the race, Lena maintained her lead, bouncing down the steady slope with blooms in hand and left arm swinging like an orchestra conductor's.

Kyle was closing fast. Employing an unusual but remarkably effective technique, he took such long strides that after completing the initial little hop the toe of his trailing boot would drag on the ground for several inches as he drew it forward. Dust flew. Somehow the distance between the ground and the top of his head remained fixed at about three feet.

Slow out of the gate, Aaron was at a disadvantage, but his gravity-defying form was unparalleled. He didn't hop; he bounded.

With the downhill slope, what they soon had was some serious speed; three racecars on a two lane road.

Kyle had just begun to make his move when suddenly and without warning, Lena stopped and shouted, "I win!"

Still clutching the stem of azalea, which was now nearly blossomless, Lena spun to her right to face the vanquished competition.

Her swinging fistful of flowers slammed into Kyle's face, dropping him instantly.

Aaron, too, was caught off guard. He had taken another of his mighty leaps just as Lena made her declaration. Try as he might, he found it impossible to stop in mid-air. Landing with his feet together less than a yard up the trail from Lena, his upper body continued forward and beyond his feet, bringing him up on his toes. He took several quick, small steps on the tips of his boots in a schizophrenic effort to apply the brakes and to get his feet in front of his center of gravity where they could do some good. With his arms extended as if he were at the low end of a pushup, he crashed into Lena, knocking her flat and taking himself down with her.

They just lay there, making no sound, not moving. Then Kyle started to chuckle. At this, Lena giggled. Soon, laughter exploded from all three. When it began to fizzle, Lena's arm shot up and the sight of the tattered azalea ignited another round of laughs.

Finally spent, they climbed to their feet and brushed themselves off. Lena turned to Kyle to apologize but then drew her hands to her mouth.

"Oh, Kyle," she moaned.

Kyle looked at Lena questioningly. She pointed at his face. Aaron looked to see what she was pointing at and then began to laugh.

Kyle wiped his nose with the back of his hand and when he checked his hand, he laughed, too.

Lena apparently didn't find it funny; she just looked at the brothers and shook her head.

Aaron handed Kyle a tissue but instead of gratitude, all he got in return was a stern warning against telling anyone. Aaron didn't hold it against him, though. If a girl had given him a bloody nose, he wouldn't want word to get out, either.

CHAPTER 13
RUDE AWAKENING

That same morning

HE HAD SLEPT long past breakfast. Sunlight streamed through a slit between the gingham curtains and hit him square in the eye, making him squint. A granola bar and an orange stared at him from the bedside table. He looked around the room as best he could without lifting his head from the pillow.

Sprawled on the bed, clad in his summer pajamas, he pondered why he ached so. Hadn't he been consistent in his attendance at the health club? *Sure had.* For a desk jockey whose notion of good nutrition is a cold beer, he didn't consider himself to be in too bad of shape. Hadn't he done okay at the tree climbing school? *Cripes, yes.* No longer panicky when suspended from a rope at heights, he could say rappelling was something he truly enjoyed. *So why do I feel like I've been run over by a truck?*

It was his wife's fault, he decided. *She made me do it*, he seethed.

"It" was yesterday's visit to the ropes course, a cross between a boot camp obstacle course and a training gym for trapeze artists. True, he had promised they would try it as a family, but he hadn't known then that before one set foot on the spider web in the sky he first had to attend ground school – an entire boring hour listening to a camp counselor explain safety equipment and practices. Surely his wife would understand his reneging when she discovered this. Plus, the pictures really didn't convey how far above ground the course was. He figured that when his wife saw it up close she'd be glad he backed out.

Whoa, was he wrong. Oh, the look she gave him when he suggested they cancel! Not to be denied the final say, he warned her that the fault would be all hers if their daughter was hurt on account of this foolishness. She just huffed and walked away.

Still, he had gone to the ropes course believing it would be a cinch, and not without good reason. He had spent the past several days systematically surveying the face of the cliff south of the camp and the ascents and descents had gone rather well, he felt. But his pride had dropped several notches by the time he made his ignominious exit from the course a few hours later.

He replayed the awful experience in his mind as he lay there, afraid to move because of the pain. He had lost count of the number of times his feet slipped off the fishnet rope ladder as he made his first, and only, climb. It left him dizzy and dripping with sweat. His ego took another blow when he saw his wife and daughter scamper like monkeys, gaily traversing the tightropes, scarcely needing the guide ropes and the safety cables.

He thought back to how he served as the day's entertainment when he botched his attempt to mimic their easy passage across the long tightrope. He knew he was supposed to stand erect and look straight ahead—he hadn't completely ignored the counselor—but knowing what to do is not the same as doing it. He had looked down.

He grimaced as he recalled how his nerves got the better of him. Burying his face in the pillow, he pictured how he must have looked, his arms on the guide rope jerking from one side to the other while his feet on the tightrope did just the opposite.

Somehow he was able to continue forward in this fashion until he reached the halfway point, when each foot suddenly slipped to either side of the rope. Instinctively, he let go of the guide rope and grabbed for the tightrope before it made contact with his crotch; realizing too late that the thing that comes naturally is sometimes the wrong thing. He momentarily straddled the rope as if he were riding a bull, wincing with pain and eyes bulging. Then he rotated over with his heels to the sky and head aimed at the ground. His helmet fell off, of course; he hadn't bothered to fasten it as instructed.

Hanging on as if his life depended on it, he managed to wrap his feet over the rope and dangle there awhile until his energy ebbed and he lost his grip. Forgetting the safety line, he screamed, believing he was a goner. Instead, he just dropped a couple of feet and hung there, spinning like the needle of a compass.

One of the camp workers fetched a ladder to get him down. Feeling like an idiot, he had stormed off to their cabin as soon as his feet touched the ground.

Water under the bridge, he told himself, only half convinced.

With trepidation, he rolled to his side. *Oh that hurt*. It seemed every muscle in his body had screamed in protest. *A man's gotta do what a man's gotta do*. He gritted his teeth, slid his lower legs out over the edge of the bed, and then pushed his upper body off the mattress while rotating his feet to the floor, trying not to bend any more than necessary. He sat on the edge of the bed for a time, steeling himself.

Don't wimp out now. Then up he went, with an audible, "Unngghh." Was there any part of him that didn't hurt, he wondered? He really hoped he would limber up as he got moving.

He shuffled around a bit and then returned to pick up the orange his wife had left on the bedside table. Under it he found a note.

> *Lena's hiking with the Gardner boys. I'm going to run into Brevard. Heard it is a cute little town not too far from here with some nice shops. Know how you like shopping. Enjoy your rest.*
>
> *Bye. L.*

At first, he was irritated that she hadn't bothered to ask if he wanted to go along, but then it sank in that he had gotten what he wanted: an entire day to himself. He grew excited as he envisioned rappelling down and coming face to face with the seal of clay. Breaking it open with a single blow, he would reach in and draw out a golden nugget worth a fortune.

His aches almost forgotten, Grady shaved and got dressed, pocketed the granola bar, and headed out the door. Bits of orange peel marked his path.

On his way to the cliff, he stopped at the dining hall to scrounge up some food so he wouldn't have to return for lunch. Although breakfast was no longer being served and the building was officially closed, he found the employee entrance unlocked.

In the vacant dining room he noticed some fruit and containers of yogurt sitting on ice. Searching for something to put them in, he went over to the utensils, pulled out the spoon holder, and dumped out the spoons, making a clatter. Then he pocketed one of the spoons, grabbed a bunch of grapes and a couple of yogurts, and moved over to the hot food line. He frowned when he saw that everything had been put away.

He walked into the kitchen, where he found two of the staff busily at work.

"May I help you?" asked one.

Eyeing the countertops, Grady replied, "Yeah, I'm going on a hike and don't want to have to traipse back here for lunch. Got anything I can take?"

"We put together sack lunches for our campers *if* we have advance notice," she instructed coolly.

Grady headed toward a refrigerator.

"We can make you a couple of sandwiches and I can grab you a bag of chips and an apple," the worker said quickly. "Will that do?"

"That will do just fine, *if* you throw in some candy bars to sweeten the deal."

The worker wordlessly communicated to her associate to package up the sandwiches and then went to grab the rest of the items. Ordinarily, candy bars and packaged chips were only available to campers on a cash sale basis, but the worker didn't demand payment for them.

Lunch sack and spoon holder in hand, Grady was soon out the door. He heard the throw of the deadbolt behind him.

He stopped to buy a cold soda from a soft drink machine which sat outside a nearby maintenance building. While waiting for the can to be dispensed, he looked up at the sun. It was above the tops of the trees. He knew he should have gotten an earlier start and faulted his wife for letting him sleep.

Finishing off the beverage before clearing the borders of the camp, Grady tossed the can aside and quickened his pace.

CHAPTER 14
MEETING CHARLIE

"WHEW! IT'S A STEAMY ONE!" Arthur remarked, as they walked out of Sally's Place, a little restaurant along their way from Raven Cliff to the state forest.

It sure is, thought Lena, now having a greater appreciation of the eatery's antique window air conditioner. The old beast had been noisy, but it worked.

She opened the car door and was hit by another blast of hot air. She couldn't wait to get to the falls.

As Arthur backed out of the parking stall, Lena thanked him for the lunch.

"Our pleasure, Lena," he replied with a smile.

Lena wished her father would take her out to eat sometime; just the two of them, so they could sit and chat like the Gardners.

"Dad, can we get in any of the waterfalls today?" Aaron asked from the back seat.

Lena held her breath. From what Aaron had told her, Arthur had a thing about waterfalls. Aaron said he guessed it might have something to do with his having to pull out too many dead or seriously injured sightseers.

"Sure," Arthur replied, to her relief. "The lower and middle falls should be fine, but don't be getting too close to High Falls. It doesn't take a very big rock to put a dent in your head.

"Okay, thanks!"

From the enthusiasm in Aaron's voice and the high-five he and Kyle exchanged, Lena could tell that the brothers considered this a victory won. She looked over the seatback and grinned.

"I know you two know this," Arthur added, "but for Lena's benefit I'll repeat it: don't be playing around the top of any of the falls. Those rocks can be slick, and if you slip and fall, it's easy to get swept over the edge."

Arthur looked over at her, so she nodded to confirm that she got the message.

Lena felt post-meal lethargy setting in, and she figured the others must have felt it, too, because the interior of the car grew quiet.

Eventually, Arthur broke the silence "What have your folks got planned for the day, Lena?"

"Mom was goin' to Brevard to do some shoppin'."

"Good place for it. And your father?"

"Uh, I'm not sure what Daddy had planned. We haven't seen him that much, really." She averted her eyes. "He must go on walks in the woods or something."

"Hmm."

Lena regretted having said so much. She didn't want Mr. Gardner to feel sorry for her, and she knew there was nothing he could do to fix her broken family. She was glad that he didn't pursue it further.

Soon, she felt the car slowing, and saw that they were approaching the entrance to the state forest.

"Boys, this might be the best time to catch Charlie," Arthur announced while eyeing the rear view mirror. "You still want to ask him about that file?"

"You bet," Aaron replied.

"Okay, to Charlie's we will go."

As Arthur turned off the highway into the parking area, Lena admired the stacked rock pillars which flanked the entrance. Slender, with perfectly square corners, and taller than a man, she wondered what kept them from toppling.

At the end of the parking area they came to a locked gate. When Arthur got out of the car to unlock it, Lena asked the brothers what Charlie did there.

"Mainly, he runs the dozer," answered Kyle.

"Oh." Lena gave a little nod as if she knew what he was talking about. She hadn't a clue.

Arthur climbed back in the car and drove through the opened gateway. As the car crept forward, one of the back doors opened. Lena turned to see Aaron hop out of the moving vehicle. After clearing the path of the metal pole gate, the car came to a stop. Lena watched Aaron run over to push the gate closed, refasten the padlock and rush back to the car. Lena wasn't sure what happened first; Aaron climbing aboard or the car getting underway. Arthur said nothing, but she saw him look into the rear view mirror and nod approvingly.

To Lena, the process appeared choreographed. She guessed it was something they had done many times. She thought of all the unspoken expectations involved in that short scene, how father and son each trusted the other to act a certain way, and neither had disappointed. It left her with a bittersweet feeling.

The service road was made of egg-sized rocks and was quite bumpy, discouraging conversation. After about three-quarters of a mile, they veered off to the right onto a narrower and even bumpier branch.

Suddenly, it felt as if the car had dropped into a huge hole. Lena's stomach leapt into her throat. They were falling into a raging river! She screamed and grabbed the dashboard.

Her amused chauffeur kept right on going. A smooth granite slab lay hidden a couple of inches beneath the surface.

"Mom wouldn't like it one bit if we took her car on this shortcut in the spring, would she boys?" The water could be two feet deep that time of year, and flowing fast enough to push a car downstream.

Lena turned and stuck out her tongue at the two yahoos in the back seat who wouldn't stop laughing.

This roller coaster shortcut soon merged into a lane walled on both sides by pines. Tall, straight, and evenly spaced, the pines formed perfect lines whether she looked directly into the forest, partly forward, or angling to the rear.

"Who...?"

Before Lena could finish asking who planted them and why, the walls suddenly opened up around them and she found herself in a huge, elongated clearing monopolized by an asphalt-paved strip.

"We're taxiing down the runway," explained Arthur, leaving her no less perplexed.

Before she could ask what a runway was doing in the middle of nowhere, a low, nasally voice intoned from the back seat: "Come in tower. Tower do you copy? Zero-one-niner requesting permission to take off from runway numero uno."

She turned to see Kyle speaking into his fist.

Mimicking him, Arthur brought his fist to his mouth. "Control tower here," he said calmly. But then suddenly in a panic, he commanded, "Negatory Zero-one-niner! You appear to have lost your wings and tailfin! Taxi to the hangar immediately! Do you copy? Zero-one-niner, *do you copy?*"

"Roger, tower; we read you loud and clear. Zero-one-niner taxiing to the hangar as instructed. 10-4. Over and out."

Kyle and Arthur "hung up" their imaginary microphones.

Throughout this exchange, Aaron had sunk further and further down in his seat.

Arthur brought the car to a stop in front of a corrugated steel building, its tall doors wide open. Instead of the airplane Lena expected to see inside, there sat an old truck. Even from inside the air conditioned car, Lena could hear the screech of a powered grinding tool coming into contact with metal.

Remaining seated, Arthur said, "Here you are kids. I've got to run over to Crystal Lake to meet a crew that came down from Asheville to refurbish the dock." He then fished out a folded piece of paper from his pocket and handed it to Aaron. "Here's a list of stuff I'd like Charlie to bring over in the next hour or so. Except for the compressor and some galvanized fasteners he was going to pick up for me in town, I've got it all laid out on the workbench. You might want to hitch a ride with him when he comes. It'd save you about a mile of hiking."

"Will do," said Aaron.

After they climbed out of the car, Arthur rolled down his window and apologized for having to rush off, confirmed the place he was to pick them up at the end of his workday, and then drove back toward the crushed rock road.

While they watched him drive away, Aaron leaned toward her and explained that this was once a boys and girls camp and that the owner had built the airstrip for his private use. "Parents must have paid a bundle, huh?" Then he offered her his arm and asked, "Shall we?"

"Let's," she replied, hooking her arm in his. Then, with a high society tilt of her head, she threaded her other arm around Kyle's, completing the chain. Thus linked, they marched toward the noisy hangar.

They entered a handyman's dream. Tools hung from the walls. Gas cans and various pieces of equipment lined the perimeter. Stacks of rough-cut lumber covered the floor on the side of the building not occupied by the truck.

Lena could see around the truck just enough to make out the back of a man sitting hunched over on a high stool in front of a workbench. So many sparks were flying out from whatever he was grinding that she was afraid he might catch fire.

Suddenly the noise and sparks stopped and the man sat straight up. There was a loud bark and the man popped up off his seat with a "Whoa, Newt!"

"Darned chili dogs," he muttered after settling back down.

Discombobulated, Lena covered her mouth with her hand. She looked at Aaron, but he just stood there with his mouth open as if he didn't know what to do."

From Kyle, however, came a staccato burst: "Who...ooo...oo's, heh, heh, heh, New...ew...ewt?" His words were intermixed with his laughter.

Lena slid behind Aaron.

Almost falling off his stool, the man made only half a turn toward them before shouting, "Crime in Italy! Why in Sam Hill are you Gardners always sneakin' up on a feller like that?"

"Hey, Charlie," greeted Aaron sheepishly.

Charlie set down the iron bar he was working on and removed his eye shield. "Where you boys been keeping yourselves?" he asked, tossing aside his gloves. "It's been so long I figured you must have gone off to war or got married or something worse."

Then the wiry man rushed over to Kyle, grabbed him around the middle and tucked him under his right arm. "As for you, I've got a barrel of sheep dip out back I've been wanting to try out on that mop of yours." He ruffled Kyle's hair with his free hand.

"Noooo," protested Kyle, still laughing.

Charlie had to be in his upper sixties and he was barely taller than Kyle but from the way he tossed him around, Lena guessed he was as tough as nails.

Charlie hadn't taken two steps with his captive before he spotted her. His eyes went wide and he set down his load.

"Pardon me. Where are my manners? I should let you boys introduce me to your friend first."

Aaron made the introduction.

"Pleased to make your acquaintance, Lena," Charlie said genuinely, adding an awkward bow.

Lena told "Mr. Barnes" that she was pleased to meet him, too, which was true, but she really wished it were under less embarrassing circumstances.

"So, what brings you all to my humble workshop this afternoon?" he asked.

Aaron told him about finding the file and then handed it to him. "Dad thought you might have an idea of what it was doing there."

Charlie examined it, turning it around in his fingers. "I see what you mean. Odd place for this to be."

"Why's it called a bastard?"

"Not quite sure, Kyle. May have something to do with how rough the teeth are, and how they are set. Could be in the olden days there were two types of teeth, and someone came up with this new cut, which wasn't purely one or t'other."

Kyle pursed his lips and nodded.

"Then again," Charlie continued, "these here bastard files are about the best things there is for sharpening really dull or dinged up mower blades. One of these files will shave those rough spots right off, but without the risk of gouging the metal, like you're apt to do with a grinder."

"I don't get it," Kyle confessed. "How does that explain the name?"

"Oh, yeah. Joints ain't the only thing that's lockin' up on me," mumbled Charlie, before further expounding on his theory. "Let's say you go to work on one of them rough blades with a regular tooth file; well, you'd be lucky to do more than polish up the dings."

"So if you've got a real bastard to work on," Aaron put in, "this file is the one to use."

"Bingo," Charlie affirmed with a wink.

Not forgetting the original question, Charlie asked if they had seen evidence of any construction or trail work in the vicinity. When they said not, he rummaged through one of the bench's drawers and pulled out something wrapped in cloth. Handling the swaddled object gently, Charlie pulled aside the folds to reveal a large magnifying glass, which he then used to examine the file for the better part of a minute.

When he looked up, he said, "It looks new, except for some spots of rock dust and a small red stain. The dust looks like it was jammed there on impact. It sure wasn't from filing on something; the crud don't extend across enough teeth. And none of the teeth show any sign of wear. The red stain isn't rust;

blood maybe. File probably hadn't been there long; doubt more'n a week."

He handed the file back to Aaron, and then concluded, "It's a mystery, boys. My best guess is some rock hound was toting it. I doubt it dropped out of a pack; I don't think it would have picked up those spots of rock dust from a little fall like that. But why somebody would ditch a perfectly good tool is beyond me. If the red stain is blood, I suppose it might have poked the fellow carrying it, riling him so much that he tossed it."

"Why would a rock hound have it?" Aaron asked.

"To help him figure out what he's dealing with," explained Charlie. "You see, minerals are not all of the same hardness. Gold and silver are about the same, but they're both harder than graphite and softer than iron pyrite, which is Fool's Gold. Diamond is really hard. Each kind of mineral has been given a hardness number; the higher the number, the harder it is. It's called the, uh, the hmmm…the Mohs scale."

"Anyway, rock hounds will use things like pennies, steel files, and pocket knife blades to estimate their sample's hardness. He will try to scratch it with the knife or the penny or whatever, and then try it the other way around; using the sample to scratch the knife blade, or the penny, and so on. He knows his fingernail is softer than a penny. A knife blade, unless it is a really good one, is about halfway up the scale. And a steel file is up a notch or so from a knife. With experience, a feller can nail down the range of hardness pretty good."

"Gosh, is that the only way to tell rocks apart?" asked Kyle.

"I'm no geologist, so I can't say for sure, but I believe the hardness test is used to identify the mineral *in* a rock, not the rock itself. A rock usually contains several minerals. But to answer your question; no, there's other things a person can look at: color; if it's crystalline; the angles of the crystals; what kind of mark it makes on a chalk-board-like doohickey called a streak plate; so on and so forth. Sometimes the mineral's easy to recognize, sometimes not. Just depends."

"How did you learn all this Charlie?" asked Aaron, obviously impressed.

"Collected rocks when I was your dad's age. Jack of all trades and master of none, as they say. Spent most of my life trying to figure out what I wanted to do when I grew up. You can learn a little about a lot that way, but I wouldn't recommend it; retirement package ain't too good."

"What did you say the name of that scale was, Charlie?" Kyle had a penchant for acquiring near encyclopedic knowledge of anything which interested him and, to the dismay of parents and teachers alike, ignoring everything else.

"Mohs," answered Charlie. "When I first heard of it, I thought of The Three Stooges. Now they just pop into my mind whenever the subject comes up. Mineral identification...The Three Stooges; Bingo! Larry's scale doesn't sound right, and neither does Curly Joe's, so that leaves Moe's. It's spelled differently, though, with an "h" instead of an "e", if I remember right."

Aaron accepted the file from Charlie's tanned and vein-crossed hand, thanked him, and relayed Arthur's message.

"Won't take long to grab the stuff," Charlie replied. "Help me load it into the truck and I'll give you a lift over to High Falls."

"Super!"

While Aaron helped Charlie gather the supplies, Kyle pulled Lena outside to show her "Katie", Charlie's World War II vintage bulldozer.

Katie was monstrous; a dark olive green behemoth. Instead of wheels, she had hinged steel drive belts like a tank. Big thick arms extended down to a huge steel curved blade which spanned the entire front. Lena could not imagine how such a small man could control such a big machine.

Yet control it he did. He could almost make the monster dance. Under Charlie's stewardship the powerful beast moved delicately and gently when necessary, and at other times like a maniac bent on destruction. He used the bulldozer to move boulders, knock down trees, remove huge tree stumps, and make roads; sometimes moving tons of earth. Arthur had often said that Charlie and his "girl, Katie," were the two most valuable workers in the forest, doing the work of hundreds of shovel and axe equipped men.

Lena accompanied Kyle as he slowly made his way around Katie. She marveled at his grasp of the hydraulic system and the bulldozer's various controls. Seeing Kyle's deep interest in the machine's inner workings made her think of her father; how different the two were.

"He said he needed it to sharpen our lawnmower blade," Lena said with a chuckle.

"Huh? Who needed what?"

"Oh, I'm sorry. I was just talking to myself. I was thinking about Daddy; how he said he needed the file to sharpen our lawnmower blade."

"What's funny about that?" Kyle looked confused.

"You'd have to know Daddy...and our mower. Daddy's not exactly handy. The last time the mower worked was two summers ago. There I am mowing the yard, when it starts smoking and whining and then just stops with a clunk. Mom comes out and after checking the oil says Daddy never put any in it. She's been paying the neighbor boy to mow the lawn ever since."

After he stopped shaking his head, Kyle asked, "Why don't you buy a new one?"

"Daddy keeps saying he's going to get the old one fixed."

Lena felt small. It embarrassed her to know how undependable her father was, yet at the same time she thought less of herself for not believing in him.

"There you are," called Aaron from the hangar's side door. He motioned for them to come. "The pickup's loaded and Charlie's ready to go whenever we are."

CHAPTER 15
GOING DOWNHILL

GRADY SCURRIED east along the path paralleling the cliff, scanning the trees for the adhesive bandage he had stuck there when he left for the ropes course yesterday. The makeshift blaze marked the place he would cut off toward the cliff to resume his search.

He had only inspected about one-half of the cliff, and he worried that he might not be able to finish the job. Camp would end in a little over two days. But then he calmed himself with the thought that he could stumble upon the mine at any time.

After finding the marked tree, Grady made a beeline for the cliff; or as much of a beeline one could make in the dense underbrush. In his haste, he made little effort to dodge pesky branches. His arms were soon crisscrossed with thin red lines. Brown patches of sweat continued to enlarge their borders on his khaki shirt, claiming most of it. Salty droplets ran down his forehead and stung his eyes.

Although he hated to take the time, he stopped to splash some water on his face, and then wet his hair and the back of his neck. He gulped down what remained in the bottle, knowing he had more stashed with his gear.

Finally, he saw the sky through the trees, which perked him up. It meant he would soon feel the cooling breeze which had welcomed him to the cliff every day since his arrival. However, when he neared the cliff, he found the air was almost perfectly still, affording no relief.

He swore.

Grady had piled his climbing gear at the base of a sturdy tree he planned to use as his next anchor, and it didn't take him long to find it. Wasting no time, he picked up his harness, stepped into it and belted in. Next, he took a loop of webbing called a "runner," wrapped it around the tree, and then linked the two ends with a screwgate carabiner. After screwing the gate down tight, forming a solid, secure oval ring, he threaded his climbing rope through it and tied it off using a rewoven figure eight knot. The rope now was securely anchored.

Grady had a fear of heights and he started to feel the jitters. He knew from experience that they might stay with him for most of the time he was working along the cliff, but so far he had managed to keep going in spite of them. He hoped that would hold true today, too.

The ropes he had brought were fifty meters in length and he had been pleased to learn that he probably would need only one of them. Although the terrain at the foot of the cliff sloped steeply downward, from the description of the mine's location he was confident that it would be found where the slope was vertical, or nearly so, and the cliff's face didn't appear to exceed fifty meters anywhere along this stretch.

Grady drew up some of the rope and tied an overhand knot, forming a small loop. Then he clipped into the loop with a carabiner which hung by a runner from his harness. This would serve as his temporary safety line while he worked near the edge.

The knowledge that he was secured to the rope helped keep him from freezing up.

Moving to the lip of the drop-off, and ignoring the visual feast spread out before him, he began to pay out the rope. He knew from experience that it was best not to toss all of it at once. It was a chore to haul up the knotted mess if it got tangled on the way down. But his impatience soon won out and he gave the rope a heave.

This time he got lucky.

Returning to his stash of gear, he grabbed a double étrier and shook it out. He initially had balked at paying so much for what he judged to be a rather flimsy looking fabric ladder, but now he considered it to be one of his wiser purchases. With it he could climb down below the rim, placing him in a better position to rappel. Also, it made it a great deal easier for him to climb back on top when he was done.

He clipped the étrier into the same loop his safety line was connected to, and then he draped it over the edge. He hated how his heartbeat raced during this part.

Next, he grabbed the ascenders and clipped them to his harness. *Almost ready to go.* Satisfied with his progress, needing to relax a bit, and not wanting to try to eat while dangling on the side of a cliff, he decided to break for lunch.

After he had eaten his fill, he tossed the trash aside with a belch and then donned his gloves and helmet. Next, he pulled up on the rope to give it some slack and tucked it into a mechanical rappelling device at his waist. This device allowed him to easily control the rate of his descent by varying the amount of tension he exerted on the "dead rope", the trailing portion which doesn't bear the climber's weight.

Finally, after checking to be sure nothing was amiss, he unhooked the safety line.

"Guess I can't put this off any longer," he remarked aloud as he straddled the rope and turned to face the anchor tree. Then he dropped down to his knees, took a couple of deep breaths, and began to back his way over the edge. Hanging onto the étrier as if his life depended on it, and being careful to not look down, he anxiously fished around with his right foot until he found one of the rungs. The left was easier. He continued stepping down.

When he felt he was in a position to safely rappel, he wrapped the dead rope around his back and grasped it securely in his right hand. To slow his descent, he would simply need to draw that hand toward his belly.

He leaned back and looked down over his shoulder to get a view of his route. It was dizzying. He estimated that he was roughly 150 feet above the base of the cliff, about the height of a thirteen-story building. Fighting the urge to turn back, he eased up on the dead rope and began to walk backwards down the cliff wall.

As had been his practice, after descending fifteen feet or so, he tied off the dead rope at his harness. This freed up his hands while he traversed the cliff in both directions. He doubted that the mine was this high up, but he thought it best not to take any chances.

When he finished with his lateral inspection, he dropped down again and repeated the process.

It became a square dance on a wall: *untie and drop, one and, two and, three and, tie-off and promenade left, one and, two and, three now back, one and, two and, three now right, one and, two and away we go.*

It grew tedious. Once he actually considered launching backwards to do a 360-degree spin, but he came to his senses and decided to rest and refocus. Tying off the dead rope, he unclipped the water bottle from his belt and took a few refreshing swigs as he hung there in the still heat. Looking down, what he saw made him doubly glad; he was almost finished with this section and he had sufficient rope.

That's odd. He heard what sounded like a stout wind blowing through leafy trees. It appeared to be coming from the west; from a canyon or recess along the mountainside. *Could it be the waterfall?* He resumed his inspection with renewed vigor.

When he had sidestepped as far left as he could, something caught his eye. A spot about thirty feet up from the base of the cliff appeared to be darker and more contoured than the surrounding rock.

He was tempted to ascend and reposition the rope to check it out but he knew if it proved to be a false lead he would have to come back down and complete this section. *No, better finish this.*

Grady returned to center and began what he hoped would be his final rappel on this portion of the cliff. He had found that three relatively short and easy drops would carry him about the right distance. The first couple of drops worked like always; he drew the dead rope toward his belly and slowed down, but on the third drop he drew the dead rope to his belly, and fell faster.

His right leg led the way into the top of the slope. His ankle twisted grotesquely inward and he heard a bone snap. A white flash blotted out his vision.

Falling backwards, he came down hard on his hip with searing pain. His back hit next, fortunately on a fairly flat layer of scree. Powerless to stop them, Grady's legs continued their arcing journey over his torso, the top of his helmeted head serving as a pivot point for the beginning of what looked to be a backward layout summersault. His entire body took flight as the momentum carried him out from the base of the cliff.

He came down hard on his face—so hard that he bounced—and then slid a few more feet before the energy of the fall was fully dissipated.

The sluice gate opened and pain came rushing in, fast and hard. He grew lightheaded; then nauseated.

None too soon, sweet blackness swallowed it all.

CHAPTER 16
BACK TO CAMP

THE TEENS were mostly dry when they climbed into the car. Aaron was glad he had suggested that they get out of the river when he did, for Arthur had the air conditioner running on max.

On the drive back to camp, Kyle excitedly told Arthur about having found a hollowed out space behind the second of the Triple Falls. About eight feet high and one hundred feet wide, these middle falls spanned the river. Kyle had gone first, piercing the watery wall near the far shore to find an indentation with a shelf deep enough to walk upon. After some cajoling, Aaron and Lena ducked in with him, and the three followed the damp, dark passage over halfway across the river before finding their way blocked.

Lena inserted that her favorite part had been looking out from behind the waterfall. They had crouched in one of the wider spots for a time, watching kaleidoscopic images of sky and forest play across the translucent flowing screen. She said it was what she guessed the Northern Lights must be like, except without the cold.

For Aaron, though he wouldn't tell it, the highlight of the afternoon had been stretching their wet selves out to dry on the sun-baked rock slab adjacent to the falls. Lying on his stomach next to Lena with his head resting on the back of his hands, he studied her face while she napped. He could imagine none prettier.

It was partly why he was feeling so lousy now. Knowing this might be the last time he saw her had his stomach in knots. It didn't help matters any that he now knew what was bothering her but felt helpless to do anything about it.

He heard his dad ask what Charlie thought about the file. Kyle, all wound up now, started to give him a summary, so Aaron returned to his reverie.

Lena had opened up to him on their way back from the falls. The two had been left alone after Kyle spurted off to prove to the "slowpokes" that he could beat them to the appointed rendezvous even if he took the long way around.

"Aaron...you remember back at the chapel?" she had asked, sounding as if she was swallowing air.

"Sure." He could tell she was not having an easy time talking about it.

"You knew I had been crying, didn't you?" It was more of a statement than a question.

He nodded.

In a voice less strained, she explained that she had been so hopeful about the trip, but it had turned into a big disappointment.

"You don't like the camp?"

"Oh, no, that's not it. The camp's great. It's just that it isn't turning out like it was supposed to. When Daddy asked us if we wanted to come here, I thought he wanted us to be a family again; to have fun together; to spend time with one another. But he's still been avoiding us, going off into the woods alone. He wouldn't even let me go hiking with him!" She started to cry.

Aaron didn't know what to say. He patted her on the back nervously, which seemed only to make matters worse, so he forced himself to stop.

When she was able to speak again, she told him about their time at the ropes course. What was to have been family fun time had become a depressing disaster.

Shuffling to a stop, she turned toward him, and then choked up again, hardly able to say the words. "Aaron, I think they're going to get a divorce....I think I'm losing my family."

Then Lena began to sob, her whole body heaving. The angelic face he had been admiring earlier was crunched in pain and fear. Never had he seen such despair, yet he felt powerless. He hurt for her.

He had wrapped his arms around her, holding her tight, hoping to somehow absorb some of her anguish. He sought for something to say which might give her hope, but nothing came so he just stood there holding her until her shuddering and sobbing stopped.

"Thought it might be something like that."

Huh? His father's comment jarred Aaron. For a second, he wondered if his dad had read his mind, but then it dawned on him that his dad was referring to Charlie's thoughts about the file.

"Where exactly did you say you found it?" Arthur asked.

Kyle began to answer, so Aaron again tuned out the conversation and returned to the time he and Lena had spent alone.

He couldn't say how long they had stood there, but when she lifted her head from his shoulder and smiled up at him he realized she had her arms wrapped around his waist. When they started on their way, they walked hand in hand. It had all been so natural, so fluid; not at all like when he was around other girls.

At the top of some stone steps they had come to a trail intersection. Overlooking the quiet junction was quaint picnic shelter. Its wooden shingles were covered with lichen, giving it the appearance of something ancient. To one side, down a short path, sat a much less romantic, but equally serviceable structure; a plastic-sided outhouse.

"Mind if I take a quick detour?" he asked, his eyes making it obvious where he planned to go.

Lena pointed behind him in the trees to their right and cried, "Look! A tufted titmouse!"

"Where?" He swiveled in that direction and scanned the trees, unsure whether he was to be on the lookout for a rodent or a bird.

When he heard her shout "Take a number!" a moment later, she already was halfway to the outhouse. With pursed lips upturned, Aaron shook his head at the memory. *Man, I'll miss her.*

The car went over a little rise and then dropped, once more jolting him back to the present. He had felt this sensation before on this road. He glanced out the window for confirmation of what he already knew. They were almost at the camp's entrance. He felt a little sick.

"I'm not quite sure," Lena began in reply to a question Aaron had not fully heard. "I think this might be the night we are to hike to the top of a bald mountain. Our camp counselor said there was to be a full moon."

"Better hope you don't run into an old screech owl," Kyle warned with a devilish grin.

"Hey, don't spoil the surprise," Arthur interjected, driving past the place where they had picked up Lena that morning. The inside of the car grew quiet.

As they continued along the road skirting the camp, Aaron stared at the back of Lena's head. His eyes felt weird; like they were in a pressure chamber. He felt the car slow.

"Lena, that's the dining hall up there off to our left, isn't it?" Arthur asked, pointing to a long, wood-sided, single-story building with a large deck extending over the steep hillside. A series of wooden stairs zigzagged up from the road to the deck.

"Yes." She answered so softly that Aaron could barely hear her.

Arthur stopped at the base of the stairs. He looked at his watch. "5:45. Fifteen minutes to spare," he announced cheerfully. But when he turned to see the faces on his passengers, his smile disappeared.

Lena unzipped a pocket of her backpack and pulled out a small notepad. She jotted something on a page, tore it out, and then handed both the page and the notepad over the seat to Aaron. "I want to get your address so I can send y'all a thank you," she explained.

Aaron looked at the loose page, cracked a smile, and carefully tucked it into his shirt pocket. He then reciprocated in the neatest hand he could muster. Feeling not at all joyful, he didn't include a happy face like the one Lena had sketched on hers.

CHAPTER 17
GOODBYE SHY GUY

ARTHUR WATCHED Aaron and Lena walk up the steps side by side while Kyle brought up the rear. He found it curious that Kyle appeared to accept his trailing place. He also noted that Kyle held Lena's backpack. *That kid*, he thought, pleasantly surprised.

Several minutes passed and his sons still had not returned. *What's taking them so long?* He began to regret having suggested that they accompany Lena up to the dining hall to get her reconnected with her parents. He gazed up at the dining hall as if this might somehow telepathically summon them back to the car.

More minutes passed with no results. *One more super power I don't have.* He stopped gazing and began to massage his neck.

Finally, after several more minutes, he noticed all three teens were standing in a huddle on the deck. Soon, his sons headed toward the steps. Aaron stopped and then Lena ran over and gave him a hug. He hugged her back. It was no little hug, either. And then….

Arthur lowered his eyes, feeling like a Peeping Tom. *Hmmm, my shy son is not so shy after all.*

When he looked up again, Aaron was bounding down the steps, already halfway to the car. Lena had moved over to the railing, waving like someone embarking on a cruise.

"Bye Kyle...Bye Mr. Gardner," Arthur heard her shout. "Thank you again!"

He smiled and waved back until his sons climbed in.

When he got the car turned around and drove past the dining hall on their way to the highway, Lena was gone.

"Got her all situated, did you boys?"

"Kind of," Aaron answered.

When his sons explained what had happened, Arthur considered going back. He later wished he had.

CHAPTER 18
A BAD BREAK

HE CAME TO with his face in the dirt. He hurt all over and felt queasy. He tried to push up off the ground but a burst of white hot pain punished him back into place. When he could think again, he resolved to avoid any sudden movements.

At least it's still daylight.

Besides hurting like the devil and feeling like he was reliving his worst hangover, he was surprised at how dry and parched he was. He tried to lick his lips but his tongue felt like sandpaper. *Water.*

Moving only his arm, he fished for the polycarbonate water bottle clipped to his waist and found it, part of it, at least. There was a big chunk missing, leaving a jagged edge. *May be why it feels damp there. Hmmm, could be blood, too. Damn.*

Careful to keep the broken side up, he slowly drew the bottle to his face and then took some deep breaths to make up for the ones he had missed. There was still some water inside! Moving his head as little as possible, he poured a little into his mouth and swished it around before swallowing. *Aaaah.*

He checked his palm. *Good.* There was not much blood, no more than could be explained by the abrasions on the heel of his hand.

He wanted to take another drink but forced himself to set the bottle aside. There was no telling how long this meager supply would have to last.

Yes, *how long?*

"Just be sure to call before you go anywhere," Grady heard his wife tell Lena anytime she went out with friends. He had felt sorry for her but now he wished his wife had made the same demands of him. Now, nobody would know where to look for him. But that had been the point, hadn't it; keeping his activities and whereabouts a secret? *Stupid, stupid, stupid.*

Sliding his hands shoulder width apart, he began what he would describe as a girly pushup—not lifting his waist off the ground. He felt it in his back, right leg and hip; but the pain wasn't excruciating. So next he tried moving from side to side, like doing prone side bends. Pushing with his left arm and pulling with his right, he slid his chest across the ground.

Bam! He was hit by searing pain; pain so intense that beads of sweat burst from his forehead; pain so severe that he couldn't be sure of the source.

For a while, he was frozen by agony and fear, but the pain eventually subsided and his paralysis along with it. He raised his arm to look at his right leg. It took awhile for his mind to register what his eyes were seeing, but when it did, waves of nausea washed over him. His arm dropped down like a shade, mercifully blocking his view.

One or both bones in his lower leg had snapped. One jagged end stuck through the thin cloth of his pants. The ivory bone sharply contrasted with the surrounding fabric, now almost black with blood. But this was not what sickened him. Instead, it was seeing the sole of his boot. His foot was folded grotesquely over his leg, as if he were some rubber Gumby.

He forced back the bile rising in his throat. Then, temporarily numbed to the pain, he lifted his head and shoulders off the ground and rested on his forearms, looking at, but not seeing, the ground in front of him.

Self-rescue obviously was not an option. Survival was the only question. *What is one to do in case of shock? Is the head supposed to be higher than the feet? Or is that heatstroke? Hah! What am I thinking?* Realizing that there was no way his head and feet were going to switch places, it gave him some comfort to know there was a fifty-fifty chance that he was in the right position.

He considered his foot. *Bent over like that, might blood flow be cut off? Is there a risk of gangrene?* His nose turned up as if he had smelled something rotten. The thought of being poisoned by his own rotting flesh scared him more than the thought of unfolding his foot. But how to straighten it? *Maybe if I flip over on my back I can sit up and wrestle it back into place.* He trembled to think about rotating his body over the jagged end of the exposed bone. If that were not deterrent enough, he pictured what would happen if his foot didn't move with the rest of his body—his lower leg would look like a towel being wrung out. *There has to be a better way.*

He scanned the ground around him. Most of the climbing rope lay in serpentine coils near the base of the cliff. The slope was covered with talus but a few feet to his left grew a large shrub, somehow thriving in its rocky setting. Some of its branches looked fairly stout.

He gingerly slid his left hand into his pants pocket, searching for his knife. No luck. He tried the pocket on the right. It stung when he rubbed the abraded hand against the rough cloth but he found the knife. He shifted it to his left hand, pried open the blade, and then pushed his upper body over a couple of inches.

He wasn't sure whether it was the stretch of his muscles or the slight movement of his injured leg, but again the pain hit like lightning. Again, strobe-like explosions flashed in his head. Again, sweat beaded on his forehead.

"God," he whimpered.

In what was a first for him, he had not uttered the word as a curse. He invoked it as a title. It was a plea for help. What he faced was too big for him, and he knew it. There was no one else to whom he could turn.

The pain eased. He began to whittle away at the base of one of the thicker stems. When every little movement could mean torture, he doubted whether he would have the nerve to go ahead with his plan, but for lack of a better idea he kept at it. Eventually, patience, perseverance and a dose of desperation paid off and the stem drooped to the ground. *Yes!*

He rejoiced too soon. The stem held on by a sinew. Tugging at it succeeded only in making his leg throb mightily. He tried twisting the stem around and around but this accomplished no more than did the tears of frustration pooling in the corners of his eyes. He quit.

After a little while, he picked up his knife and sawed at the stubborn strip of bark. In three seconds it was severed. He celebrated with a sip of water.

Next, he started trimming off branches. He found that it didn't give him too much pain if he took it a little at a time and shaved off thin slivers instead of trying to power through the wood in a few slices.

When he came to a suitably thick branch about three feet up the main stem he stopped trimming and went to work on the branch and the stem, cutting both off several inches above the junction. The finished product resembled a stubby shuffleboard stick.

Exhausted, he closed his eyes and tried to rest but once his mind was off task the pain again took center stage. The throbbing wasn't as intense but the hurt was more constant, like a whole body headache times ten.

Better get to it, Grady thought ruefully, briefly considering whether to make it quick or to go slow and steady. Grabbing the stick firmly in his right hand he whipped his arm to his side, slid the prongs under his upturned boot, and raised his thigh while pushing down fast and hard on the stick.

He passed out to the sound of his own scream.

CHAPTER 19
A CALL IN THE NIGHT

HEARING THE PHONE RING, Arthur checked his watch. Already after nine. Wondering where the evening went, he looked up to be sure Sandra was answering it.

He saw Sandra looking at him from across the room while pointing at the phone and mouthing the words, "It's Lena." Then she carried the phone down the hall. He assumed she was taking it to Aaron. He had seen him earlier, sprawled out on his bed, moping.

Arthur considered getting up to witness his son's mood swing, but he decided against it.

Ten minutes later and Aaron was standing in front of him, anxiously relating what Lena had said. His son's mood had changed alright, but not in the way Arthur expected.

Lena's father was missing.

A man from the city out alone in the woods without having told anyone where he was going—Arthur disliked hearing such news. Knowing that it involved Lena, he liked it even less; and not just because they knew her. After dropping her off at camp, he discovered that neither of Lena's parents had been waiting for her. The girl had eventually persuaded his sons to go, assuring them that her parents would be there soon. Arthur already felt guilty about having left her alone. *And now this....I should have gone back.*

"They don't have any idea where he may have gone?" Arthur asked to be sure.

Aaron shook his head and then added, "Just on a hike, is all. I asked Lena to look for marked maps or any papers that might give us a clue."

"Good thinking. They happen to check to see if their car is still there?"

"Yes." Aaron sounded irritated. "Lena's mom had it all day."

"Oh, yeah. She went to Brevard." After a brief pause, Arthur asked, "How about his suitcase?"

"Still there, and believe me, this is something you do *not* want to ask Lena about."

"She's a little sensitive about it, huh?"

With his eyes opened wide and lips pursed tightly, Aaron affirmed with an exaggerated nod.

Arthur knew it was too soon to start an official search and there was little more that could be done until daylight. Bloodhounds could work in the dark, but none of the good ol' boys he knew would want to waste his dog on some city dweller who had "done gone off and got hisself lost in the woods," at least not before giving the misplaced gent a day or two in the wilderness to gain some smarts. Thankfully, it was warm enough that surviving the night should not be a problem, provided he wasn't severely ill or injured.

He looked up at Aaron from his chair. "Call Lena back and get a good description of Mr. Summerlin: his date of birth, height, weight, hair color, hair length, what he was wearing; the works. If she found anything that might give us an idea where he went or what he's up to, get that, too. And tell her I'll try to get in touch with the camp director yet tonight. Other than that, there isn't much one can do until daylight. Let her know we'll be coming at dawn to help any way we can."

Aaron beamed.

"One more thing: Ask her to call if her dad shows up, regardless of the time. I don't want to run over there at that hour just to find him sleeping." Then he added with a grin, "Don't tell her I said that last part, though."

Grinning back, Aaron gave him a quick nod before vanishing down the hall.

Fetching his cell phone, Arthur scrolled through its directory and found the number he was looking for. In a moment the phone began to ring. Someone with a gruff or groggy deep voice answered unintelligibly. Arthur plunged ahead.

"Mac? Arthur Gardner here." Arthur had met Kelly McIntyre, the camp's director, a couple of years earlier at a trail building seminar.

Still a little groggy, the voice replied, "Art…why are you calling at this hour?"

Arthur checked his watch. Half past nine. His eyebrows rose with his shoulders, but he refrained from asking why the man was already in bed. *For all I know he was up all night tending to some sick kid or turd-wrestling plugged toilets all day.*

"Sorry about the wake-up call, Mac, but something has come up."

"No problem. What is it?"

Arthur told him about Lena's call but didn't identify the Summerlins by name.

"Yeah, glad you called. Wonder why they didn't call me?"

He didn't even ask the man's name. Arthur bristled at the notion of a camp administrator being more concerned about some supposed chain of command than the fact that one of his campers was missing, but then he chided himself for rushing to judgment. *Maybe he's just thinking that it must be a false alarm. Cut him some slack.*

He was glad he did, for the next thing the director asked was the man's name. Then he assured Arthur that he would go to the Summerlin cabin right away. Arthur told him of their plans to arrive at the camp at dawn to begin a search. The call concluded with an agreement to meet at the camp's dining hall at first light.

Arthur then went to find Aaron to check on his progress. He walked into the bedroom just as Aaron was getting off the phone. Placing his hand on his son's shoulder, he asked what he had learned.

Aaron rattled off the salient facts: Lena's mother was upset with her for having called them, there was still no sign of Mr. Summerlin, Mrs. Summerlin hadn't found the camp director but had spoken with a camp counselor who said he would be on the lookout for her husband.

"What about a description?"

Aaron handed him a piece of paper. Arthur looked it over. It included everything he had asked for except for what the man was wearing.

Arthur was about to ask when Aaron said, "His hiking boots are missing, but they aren't sure what else he had on."

"Good job, Bud." He gave his son a squeeze on the shoulder and then headed toward the door.

"Oh, and Dad, Lena found an old map with her dad's things, but she doesn't think it's a trail map."

"Okay," Arthur replied, only half-listening as his thoughts had turned to who else he should notify.

In the hallway, he did an about-face and called back toward the bedroom. "Aaron, go get your brother. You two need to hit the sack. We'll need to be up by five if we're going to make it to camp by sunup."

CHAPTER 20
SEARCH PARTY

THE YELLOWISH TINT to the sky behind the South Carolina foothills testified to the coming dawn but the sun had not yet peeked over the ridgeline when the Gardners arrived at camp.

The spark plugs who had climbed into the pickup in the dark chill of the morning were gone, replaced by two comatose fellows who didn't appear to have an ounce of energy between them. Aaron's head rested on a scrunched up sweatshirt stuffed against the window frame. His neck was arched back and his mouth wide open. Kyle rested on Aaron, drooling on his shirt.

Arthur pulled over to park in a wide spot along the circle drive behind the dining hall. "What happened to my bright eyed and bushy-tailed boys?" he asked, jiggling Kyle a little bit, which also jiggled Aaron.

Eyes still closed, Kyle sat upright, hunched his shoulders to his ears, yawned like a lion, and then gave his head a quick little shake.

Aaron grimaced as he straightened his neck and rotated his head in ever-widening circles. Then he stretched his arms to the limit, his intertwined fingers masochistically pulling his wrists back at right angles. Alert enough to know he was being watched, he grinned back at his dad through the slits in his crunched face.

Kyle wasn't grinning at anyone.

"Just leave your gear in the truck," their father instructed. "We'll go meet up with Mr. McIntyre and get an update."

Beckoned by the light above the doorway, Aaron walked with Arthur to the staff entrance. They waited by the door for Kyle, who had his eyes closed and was bringing up the rear in serpentine fashion. Somehow sensing when he veered off track, he would crack open one eye just long enough to get his bearings, and then set off on a corrected course.

Aaron admired his little brother for the lengths he would go to earn some extra shuteye.

When Kyle arrived, they moved inside and wound around in semi-darkness to a brightly lit work area at the far end of the kitchen. A woman was already busy taking food out of the freezer and did not notice their approach. Arthur did not disturb her, but instead went over to the serving counter and looked into the dimly lit dining room.

Alone at a round table nearest the counter sat a huge bear of a man, his hands wrapped loosely around a cup of steaming coffee. With Aaron and Kyle trailing him like ducklings, Arthur backtracked to a nearby swinging door and led them through it.

"Mornin' Mac," greeted Arthur.

The big man looked up. Even from this distance, Aaron could tell he hadn't shaved.

"Art, good to see you again." Lumbering out of his chair the man extended his hand, and he and Arthur exchanged a firm handshake.

"Mac, I'd like you to meet my two sons, Aaron and Kyle. Boys this is Kelly McIntyre, the camp director."

Aaron shook his hand first. He felt dwarfed by the figure whose hardened paw swallowed his.

Director McIntyre invited them to take a seat while he got them something to drink. "Hot chocolate okay for you fellows?" he asked, eyeing the brothers.

"You bet," answered Aaron for the both of them. "Thanks!"

While the director fetched the drinks, Arthur pulled out a topographic map from his back pocket and spread it out on the table. He hadn't studied it long before a steaming cup of coffee appeared in front of him.

"You may need to doctor up this battery acid;" their host warned, gesturing toward a basket filled with packets of sugar and powdered creamer. "The plastic cream takes the edge off."

Aaron immediately checked his drink to make sure that it was more chocolaty than his father's. Out of the corner of his eye, he saw Kyle eyeball his cup, too.

The director settled back in his seat and filled them in on the latest. After Arthur's call last night, he had gone over to the Summerlin cabin and found a very distraught woman. He had waited up with her for about an hour. Linda Summerlin told him she hadn't found a note. Something about the way she said it made him think she was referring to a "Dear John" letter, or in this case, a "Dear Jane" one.

He then looked directly at Arthur and asked how well he knew the family. Reading between the lines, it seemed to Aaron that the director suspected that the man simply had decided to leave his family.

Arthur admitted they only knew them through their daughter, Lena, and had not met her father but he added that family camp did not seem like the time a man would pick to leave. Too, he understood they had one vehicle and that Mrs. Summerlin had taken it to Brevard the day the man went missing.

The director countered that it was hard to stay lost for long. Trails would eventually tie into logging roads leading to bigger roads and then to civilization. "This isn't darkest Africa, you know."

"You've got a point," conceded Arthur. "Normally one does a systematic grid search but with just the few of us it's probably best to focus on locations a day hiker is apt to get seriously lost or injured. Can you think of anyplace around here that might lure a day hiker off the trail and into a maze or dangerous terrain?"

"No, not really. I tend to stick close to camp on the well-beaten path, but two guys who can help you are Zach Green and Frank Culbertson. Zach's a counselor here and Frank's our volunteer handyman. They've traipsed all over this area. Zach should be here anytime now but Frank usually doesn't get here until about nine. He lives on the outskirts of Greenville so he has quite a drive. I've cleared both to join you today. I'm sorry I can't spare more, but we've got paying campers we need to take care of."

"Understood."

While the men discussed other logistics, more of the kitchen crew arrived and breakfast preparations shifted into high gear, evidenced by the increasing din.

Arthur turned to his sons. "Why don't you boys run over to the Summerlin cabin and see if Lena wants to join us or whether she's going to stay with her mother. If she wants to come, be sure she has what she'll need for a full day of hiking and then hustle back here so she can get a good breakfast before heading out."

Finally. Aaron had wanted to shout that all this talk wasn't getting them anywhere. From the way Kyle had been fidgeting, he guessed he felt the same.

"Men, have you been to their cabin before?"

It took Aaron a second or two to realize that the director was addressing him and Kyle. "Uh, no."

"Let me show you the way," he began, rising from his chair, "or our search party may go missing, too."

CHAPTER 21
MISSION CONTROL

NOW ALONE, Arthur tuned out the clamor in the kitchen and turned his attention to the map. Working out from the camp, he circled headwaters of creeks and areas where several contour lines squeezed together. These were places where one could expect abrupt changes in the lay of the land. He checked carefully for places where thin blue lines crossed the latter, as this could indicate a waterfall. He knew these were one of the deadliest hazards in the forest. Most at risk were those foolhardy ones who would wade out to the lip to take a look. It was too easy to lose one's footing on the surprisingly slick rocks lining the streambed and then get pushed over the edge by the current.

After scanning a radius of seven miles from the camp, he stopped drawing circles, doubting Mr. Summerlin would have walked any farther than this. Looking up, he saw that campers had begun to filter in and make their way through the serving line. He checked his watch. *Already past seven.* He had hoped the search would be well underway by now, but he knew that a little advance preparation could save a lot of wasted effort. Arthur folded the map and walked toward the door, but before he got through it, a tall and thin young man with brown hair rushed in, bumping into him.

The young man let out a stream of apologies.

"Zach, by chance?" Arthur interrupted.

"Mr. Gardner?"

"You found me." Arthur wore a big grin. "I was just going out to get my handy-talky. I'll be right back, but while I'm gone would you mind taking a look at this topo and see what you think about the places I've circled? I've tried to pick places a hiker is apt to go and get lost or hurt, but the map's been my only guide. You've got experience on the ground."

"Sure, be glad to."

Arthur thanked him and headed to the pickup. He was about there when he saw his sons and Lena jogging toward him. They met at the truck.

"Good morning, Mr. Gardner," Lena greeted between gulps of air.

"Morning, Lena. It's good to see you again, but I wish it were under better circumstances. I take it there is still no sign of your father."

She shook her head.

"Your mother is okay with your joining us today?"

"Yes. She said I could go so long as I didn't get lost. I promised I wouldn't."

Arthur smiled with her. "We'll hold you to it."

"She also told me to tell you thank you from the bottom of our hearts for what y'all are doing."

"We're glad to help."

Lena bent over her pack and started to rummage through it. "I brought that map of Daddy's in case you wanted to see it."

"Uh, sure." It didn't immediately register what map she was referring to.

Lena withdrew a folded paper from her pack and handed it to him. "I don't know if it will help or not."

Arthur unfolded it to find a photocopy of a hand-drawn map depicting the region where Georgia and the Carolinas converged. Based on the penmanship and obscurity of some of the place names, he tended to believe the original was very old, but the map's inclusion of an inset—something which he had thought to be a modern development—made him less sure.

He couldn't see how it would help them, though. The map didn't show any hiking trails and it didn't have any "X marks the spot" like one would expect on a treasure map. There was a curious large-lipped, egg-shaped face inside the inset, but he had no clue what it might signify.

He looked at his sons. "You guys got any idea of what this might mean?" He pointed to the little face.

They just shook their heads.

"Lena?"

"No. No idea."

"Do you know why your father had this?"

"No, I never saw him looking at it and he never mentioned it. I'm sorry."

Wanting to spare the girl further interrogation, Arthur looked at Aaron. "Did you ask Mrs. Summerlin about it?"

Lena broke in. "Mom said she hadn't seen the map before; she didn't know where Daddy might have got it or what he was doing with it."

"Well, it's interesting, but I'm not sure whether it means anything." He handed it back to her. "Better hang on to it, though."

Arthur turned to his sons. "Zach Green, the camp counselor who will be joining the search, is in the dining hall looking over the topo. Why don't you go introduce yourselves. I'll be in in a minute."

"When are we going to get started?" Kyle asked.

"Shouldn't be too much longer. It takes awhile to get organized and one of the things that needs doing," he said sternly, "is to get Lena her breakfast."

Kyle hurried to catch up to Aaron and Lena.

If he thinks today is bad, just wait, thought Arthur, grabbing the handy-talky from under the front seat. Last night he had phoned his friend, John Colbert, a South Carolina park ranger who was in charge of a state wilderness area south of the camp. He knew that if Ranger Colbert was successful, tomorrow searchers from the three North Carolina counties that converged near this spot would descend on the camp. Coordinating the three teams could prove challenging.

This reminded him that he needed to alert Kelly McIntyre to tomorrow's expected arrival of the Search and Rescue teams—SAR for short. It also made him think of all the trouble and expense that would be saved if they found Mr. Summerlin today.

Returning to the dining hall, Arthur found the others sharing a table. While his sons and Lena worked on their breakfasts (the brothers' second that morning), he and Zach discussed the map.

One of the first things they agreed upon was that a search of the cliff area could wait. Although it posed some danger, they doubted a casual hiker would wander that far off the trail. Too, Zach said that in daylight a person would see he was nearing a cliff in plenty of time to avoid it. For Arthur, the main consideration was one he wouldn't voice: if the man had fallen over the cliff he wouldn't need rescuing; recovering a body was a task best left to others.

When he felt he was ready, Arthur divided the search area into three roughly pie-shaped sections.

"Do you have a hand-held GPS, Zach?" Arthur asked.

"Yes, back at my cabin."

"With mine and Aaron's, that makes three; one per team," began Arthur. "I'd like have each GPS programmed so it will guide each team to its assigned search sites. Frank Culbertson is going to be joining the search, I believe, but he's not expected until around nine. If you could pair up with him, that would give you time to get your gear together and to enter your team's assigned sites into your GPS. Sound like a plan?"

"Yep, sounds like a plan," agreed Zach.

"While the kids are finishing up, why don't we go outside and see if we can't get our handy-talkies to communicate? While we're at it, we can get the coordinates of the places your team will be checking."

The two men stood to go but before leaving, Arthur said, "Aaron, if you give me your GPS, I'll enter some search sites for you and Lena,"

Aaron sat up straight. "Me and Lena?"

Arthur had hardly begun to nod before Aaron dropped his fork with its credit card-sized piece of syrup-slathered waffle, ripped the GPS from its holster and shoved it at him.

Once outside on the deck, Arthur and Zach adjusted their radios to a channel sharing a clear signal.

"If it's alright with you, Zach, I'd like to give your radio to Aaron. Then when Frank gets here you two will be able to use his."

"That'll work." Zach handed his radio to Arthur.

"Thanks. I've got one more request, but I didn't want to ask in front of Lena."

"Shoot."

"I assume the camp has an all-terrain vehicle."

"Yeah, a four wheeler."

"Since you've got some time before Frank gets here, I was hoping you could take the ATV and make a quick pass down the wider trails and logging roads around here on the off-chance Mr. Summerlin had a heart attack or stroke."

"Good idea."

"Great. Before you go, let's get you the coordinates of your search sites."

Arthur's global positioning device, or GPS, with the "S" referring to the system of satellites which enable the device to triangulate one's position with remarkable accuracy, was equipped with a detailed topographic map of this entire region. Zooming in on the area assigned to team Zach, Arthur used the device's cursor to pinpoint one of the search sites. The GPS displayed the exact coordinates of that location, which Arthur had the device "memorize" under a name he assigned, in this case "LOC1Z," short for "Location #1, Zach." Arthur also recorded the coordinates in his pocket notebook.

This Arthur did for each of the search sites assigned to Zach and Frank. When he was done, he tore out the page and handed it to Zach. "You know how to use these, don't you?"

"Sure, my little buddy's my best friend."

Arthur grinned. "Okay. Be safe out there. We'll plan to see you and Frank back here around seven, if not before."

After Zach left, Arthur went back to programming the search coordinates into his and Aaron's GPS devices. As was his practice, he also had each device "mark", or memorize, its present location, just in case a team needed help finding its way back to camp. As he was finishing up, Aaron walked over.

"About got it?" Aaron asked.

"Yep, all set," said Arthur, handing him his GPS and Zach's radio.

While Aaron holstered the equipment, Arthur checked his watch again. It was a little past eight. He glanced at the sun. It had risen above the line of haze blanketing the lower hills. The sky was fully awake now; the dawn's buttery yellow having changed to blue-white. Instinctively, he factored in the absence of wind, the rise in temperature, and the density of the haze. Extrapolating into the afternoon, he surmised it would be a miserable combination of too hot and too humid—an ordinary summer's day.

In the distance, he heard a small motor revving up. *Must be Zach.* He looked toward the dining hall entrance just as Lena and Kyle were walking out.

"All full up?" he asked when they drew near.

Kyle belched, causing Lena to giggle.

"Pardon me," Arthur said.

"For what?" Kyle asked.

"Never mind," Arthur exhaled, wondering why the Bible admonished fathers not to exasperate their sons instead of the other way around.

Shepherding them to a picnic table, Arthur spread out the topographic map and oriented it using his compass. He quickly explained the plan to split up in pairs, showed them the search "pies," and gave them a brief overview of why the assigned sites had been picked. He then assumed the efficient, businesslike tone characteristic of firearms instructors, dive masters, and others of that ilk.

"Okay, listen up," he began, and proceeded to deliver a "be safe; we won't be doing Mr. Summerlin any favors if one of us gets hurt" speech. "Any questions?" he asked at the end.

Nobody spoke.

"Okay. All teams are to be back here by seven, even if you're not finished. Understood?"

Everyone nodded.

"Alright, let's go find Lena's dad."

CHAPTER 22
LYING LOW

WHEN HE CAME TO, he saw that the sun had crept over the tops of the trees down slope. It told him that a day, maybe more, had passed since the accident. Even so, he yearned to return to the bliss of oblivion. His slightest movement caused the nauseating ache festering in his leg to radiate though his entire body. Could a broken leg cause his jaw to hurt and his head to ache, he wondered?

His tongue was dry and swollen. It stuck to his palate, making a "splack" when he pulled it loose. He tried to lick his lips but his tongue wouldn't cooperate. The sides of his mouth were crusty. Trembling, he carefully brought the broken water bottle to his lips and captured the last of its contents. A pittance, there was barely enough to dampen his mouth, much less swallow, though he painfully tried.

He looked at his leg. His self-doctoring appeared to have done some good. The sole of his boot now faced down. No longer did his leg bone protrude through his pants. Would that it had been a bad dream, but the dark stain around the tear in his pant leg testified otherwise.

He found his stick and used it to gently probe his leg. Although he took great care, when the tip of the stick touched the offending bone a spasm of pain jolted his entire body. He cried out. Tears leaked from his eyes and even his nose.

Where are they? Why haven't they found me? He couldn't understand why he wasn't hearing helicopters or an army of searchers crashing through the woods. Panicking, he tried to shout for help, but with his parched throat he sounded like a cat coughing up a hairball.

After he calmed down, he realized that no would have had any reason to worry until the previous evening—assuming it was yesterday he had fallen. *It takes some time to organize a search, too,* he allowed.

Or maybe they're keeping me waiting just to teach me a lesson. Eyebrows furrowed, he imagined what they would say when they finally showed up. *"This would not have happened if you'd had a buddy, if you'd told someone where you were going, if…, if…, if…."* A wave of anger swept him up just as the wave of panic had, but finally it, too, passed.

To keep his mind occupied, he began to hum "Waltzin' Matilda." Occasionally, some of the lyrics would occasionally pop out amid his hums—terms like "jolly swagman," or phrases like "sprang into the billabong." This intrigued him, since not only had he not heard the song in years, he had no idea what those words meant.

The diversion seemed to be helping, so he hurriedly latched on to another tune, "Hey, Jude." His humming vibrated his sinuses and tickled his nose. He could almost hear the Beatles.

It was nice for a while, but eventually he was unable to ignore the throbbing. The music stopped. He dropped his head and drew his hands into white-knuckled fists. He shut his eyes so tightly that it flared his nostrils and lined his forehead with deep creases. Through clenched teeth, he once more called upon God. It came out as a pleading groan.

Even as he prayed, he knew that there was no reason He should listen.

CHAPTER 23
DETAILS, DETAILS

ARTHUR AND KYLE started with the closest of their assigned sites and moved outward. They were now climbing up from Infirmary Rock, a cluster of huge boulders rumored to have served as a makeshift hospital for wounded Confederate deserters. They had seen no signs of anyone having been there recently. Progress reports from the other teams had been no more encouraging.

Arthur preferred projects which could be completed quickly or where progress was at least evident. He kept telling himself that they hadn't been at this very long, as such searches go, and that they *were* making progress—they now knew where Mr. Summerlin *wasn't*. But he was getting worried. It was already midafternoon, and the more time that went by without finding him, the likelier it was that he was badly injured, or worse.

"Who's checking the trail to the waterfall, Dad?"

Arthur's breathing was labored, his response coming between intermittent huffs. "The one you boys took the other day? Zach figured it got enough camper traffic that our efforts would be better spent elsewhere. Why do you ask?"

"Yesterday, Lena said something about her dad having a file like the one we found. I was wondering if he might have been rock hunting down there."

"Rock hounding, you mean?" Arthur regretted it the instant he said it. He knew that when it came to correcting his sons he could be both too quick and too critical, a disheartening combination.

"Yeah," Kyle responded, less life in his voice.

Arthur gestured at a fallen tree conveniently situated along the trail and the two sat down to take the weight off their legs.

"I kind of doubt it," Arthur answered. "From what I gathered, Mr. Summerlin isn't much for the outdoors. But it wouldn't hurt to find out if he's got an interest in that sort of thing. Why don't you check with Lena the next time you get a chance?"

Kyle said, "Yeah, I'll do that." Then after a short pause, he asked, "What if he does?"

"Well, then I'd say we ought to go take a closer look around where you found the file. Maybe he was scratching in the dirt along that hillside."

Kyle nodded. "Exactly what I was thinking."

Arthur thought of that old map. *Might it explain why some guy from Georgia would come to this out of the way place and make himself scarce almost the entire time he was here? Could he be prospecting for something?* Then he gave his head a little shake. *Gads, how a body's mind wanders.*

He spread the topographical map on the ground and then radioed the other teams to get a status report. While he was talking to Aaron, Kyle gestured to him.

"Uh, hang on, Aaron. I think Kyle wants to talk."

Kyle asked to speak to Lena and then asked if her father was a rock hound, "...you know, interested in things like gems and minerals."

"Well?" Arthur asked when it was over.

Kyle looked down and just shook his head.

"It was a good thought, anyway."

Arthur ruminated over the map a while longer, and then radioed Zach again.

"Zach, I think it's apt to take Aaron and Lena longer to finish up than the rest of us, but we could even things out if you and Frank could cover the trail to the old moonshiner's still. What do you think?"

"Can do. We won't be far from it when we're at Cascade Falls."

Arthur thanked him, and then sought confirmation from Aaron that he had heard.

"Yep, got it," said Aaron. "No partying for Lena and me."

Briefly befuddled, Arthur eventually toggled his radio but he didn't know what to say.

CHAPTER 24
DISTILLING THE CLUES

"I'M GLAD we got to cross Bootlegger's Hollow off our list," Lena said between breaths. "I don't think I could have made it."

"Yeah, I'm pretty beat, too."

Winded from having just hiked up a long incline to the top of a rise, Lena and Aaron were on their way back to camp after checking the last of their assigned sites.

"Are there are still moonshiners in these hills?" she asked.

"Not as far as I know, but I suppose it's possible."

"Is it true they shoot first and ask questions later?"

"What makes you think that?"

Lena shrugged. "Maybe something I saw in an old movie."

"These days, I'd guess it's more likely one would stumble onto somebody's marijuana patch, but I never heard of anybody getting shot over it."

Lena looked around. "How would anybody ever know if they did?"

Aaron smiled and let out a little laugh.

They hadn't gone more than thirty feet before Aaron pulled up short and grabbed Lena's forearm. "Did you hear that?" he whispered.

"No, I didn't hear anything," she whispered back.

They stood in a hushed huddle. Finally, Aaron let go of Lena's arm. "Sorry," he said. "I thought I heard voices but I guess I was hearing things."

They resumed walking, but with no conversation. Their eyes scanned the hillsides even more than before. Suddenly, they froze and looked at each other, wide-eyed. Aaron *had* heard voices and they were getting louder. The best he could tell, they were coming from behind them; from the woods off to the southeast.

Lena threaded her left arm under Aaron's right and gripped his hand tightly in hers; so tightly that her fingernails dug painfully into the flesh above his knuckles.

Then Aaron spotted them: two figures advancing briskly through the trees. *They're coming right at us!*

Aaron knew that a tug on Lena's hand was all it would take to get her to join him in making a run for it, but he doubted they would get very far; all afternoon she had continued to wind down. So he held his ground, with Lena at his shoulder, telling himself that they were probably just two guys out for a hike.

Suddenly, a grin of recognition washed over his face and Lena released his hand. Neither of them said a word as the intruders approached.

Arthur and Kyle were moving fast, with eyes on the ground. They showed no sign of knowing he and Lena were there.

The speedsters had closed to about twenty feet when Arthur's head came up momentarily, dropped down, and then popped right back up.

"Well, hello!" he blurted. "Didn't expect to run into you out here. What happened to your radio?"

"Huh?" Aaron looked down at the radio. "Oops, I must have shut it off. What did we miss?"

"I'll tell you at the next rest stop." Arthur motioned them forward.

"Any news about Daddy?" Lena pressed.

"No; no word yet. But Zach and Frank are still out looking. Not to worry; we're not giving up. Just a little change in the battle plan, is all."

Aaron saw that his dad was breathing hard, and that sweat glistened on his face and arms, darkening his shirt in spots. It concerned Aaron that he didn't want to take the time to rest.

Kyle took the lead on the footpath Aaron and Lena had been following. He set a fast pace. Aaron darted in front of Lena so he would be in a better position to slow down his jackrabbit of a brother. Arthur brought up the rear.

Aaron would occasionally look over his shoulder to check on Lena. She did fine at first, but while they were tackling another hill, he noticed that with every step she was putting a hand atop her thigh to help push off. *Not a good sign.*

A few minutes later, Arthur called loudly, "Boys. Hold up. Let's rest."

Kyle stopped and stood with his hands on his hips, stretching his neck and catching his breath. He did not turn around. Lena plunked down right where she was, and Aaron sat next to her.

Arthur came over and stood in front of them. Dropping his pack, he wiped his brow with a handkerchief. "Phew, it's a hot one. How you doing, Lena?"

She looked at him with a crooked little smile. "Okay, but my legs feel like marshmallows."

Aaron nodded. He knew just how she felt. Last year, his Phys. Ed. instructor had the class run a piggyback race, and had paired Aaron with a beefy classmate who outweighed him by at least forty pounds. Aaron made it all the way across the gym floor and was about halfway back when his legs buckled. There was no pain; they just turned to mush.

"I have just the medicine," said Arthur, pulling from his pack a packet of electrolyte-replacement drink mix and tossed it to Kyle, who by then had joined them. "Mix that for Lena, will you Kyle? I need to visit with Aaron a minute about where we go from here. If you need some water, you can get it from the hydration bladder in my pack." Then, after giving Aaron a hand up, he turned to Lena. "Drink the whole quart, if you can," he prescribed. "It's guaranteed to put zip in your bones."

"Thanks Mr. Gardner. I could use some zip."

When they were out of earshot, Arthur told Aaron that Kyle had said something which made him decide to cut short their search and head back to camp. From what Kyle told him, Arthur gathered that not only had Mr. Summerlin recently purchased a file, but he had lied to Lena about why he wanted it.

"I knew he had just bought a file that Lena thought looked like the one we found," interrupted Aaron, "but I didn't...." Aaron's comment was cut short when he heard Lena giggle. He glanced in her direction before completing his thought. "I didn't know the part about the mower."

"Yeah, I wouldn't have known it either had Kyle not been grousing about the guy not taking care of his equipment. Anyway, between the map and everything else, I'd bet the file you found was Mr. Summerlin's and that he's looking for something over there."

"To the east of the waterfall, where that face is on the map?"

Arthur nodded.

Aaron met his eyes. *Now I know why dad pulled me aside.* The chances of finding Mr. Summerlin alive had plunged.

"I'd hoped to get back and check as much of that area as we could before we lost our light, but it's not looking too good. Got any thoughts?"

"You're thinking the base of the cliffs, right?"

"Well, given the time, I was thinking about the best we could do was to check the top, but, frankly, I doubt that's where we'll find him."

"What about Ranger Colbert?"

Arthur shook his head. "Talked to him last night. He and most of his staff were going to be at some seminar in Columbia all day. Plus, it's a little too soon to call out the troops."

After pondering it a bit, Aaron's head began to bob. "I think I know a way we can get down to the base of the cliffs and make a quick sweep before dark."

"Shoot."

"I checked the map the other day before Kyle and I rode our bikes over here, and I remember seeing a trail going down a shoulder all the way to the foothills. It was two or three miles east of camp; so probably not too far from where we are now. Kyle and I could get to it in no time. We'd take the trail partway down, cut back to the base of the cliffs, and then hike along them until we reached a stream. We could follow it up to the waterfall. It would be a *cinch* to get to the camp from there."

Before Aaron finished, Arthur had pulled out his topographic map and started to unfold it.

"A cinch, huh?" Arthur said, not sounding convinced. "That's some rugged hiking and you two have been going at it pretty long already. Are you sure you can handle it?"

"I know we could. We'd take a radio and as much water as you can spare; so we'd have plenty."

Arthur quietly studied the map. He didn't have to say anything; Aaron could read his expressions like a book. His dad's raised eyebrows signaled that he was mildly surprised to see there really was a trail down the shoulder. The almost imperceptible slow bobbing of his head which followed a few seconds later told Aaron that he had decided it just might work. Aaron tried not to grin.

"When you were hiking to the waterfall did you take a look to see what the stream looked like further down?" Arthur asked.

"Yeah, but I couldn't see much. There's not much water flowing this time of year, though, so I think we could walk up the stream, if we had to."

"Hmm."

His dad turned toward the sun and held one hand on top of another in front of his face, kind of like the monkey who saw no evil. Aaron knew that he was counting the number of fingers that fit between the horizon and the sun. Allotting fifteen minutes per finger would give him a rough idea of how much time they would have before the sun dropped below the mountains. Aaron saw his dad's forehead crease.

"It's going to get dark sooner down there, you know." His dad was looking him right in the eyes.

"I know."

"And if you do find Mr. Summerlin, it may not be very pretty."

Aaron leaned toward him and lowered his voice. "Dad, I really want to do this."

His father's eyes signaled that he understood. "Okay, you two get a move on."

CHAPTER 25
RUNNING OUT OF TIME

HOT SPOTS had started to form on the soles of his feet. Aaron knew he ought to apply some duct tape but he didn't want to take the time, even if it meant paying the price in blisters. He had hoped they would be making their way across the base of the cliffs by now, but they weren't even close.

He doubted that his dad would want to hear about how hard the trail had been to find (it proved to be little more than a deer path), or about how a mass of rhododendron had overgrown the trail and caused them to temporarily get off track, or about how the map didn't depict this succession of steep switchbacks. *He will just expect us back before dark; no excuses.*

"When are we going to head for the cliff?" Kyle asked as they passed by each other at one of the switchbacks.

"Let's check." Aaron stopped to see where the GPS indicated they were in relation to where the contour lines marking the base of the cliff intersected the trail.

"We're almost at the cut-off point."

"About time."

"Yeah; I hear you."

Aaron started to look for a place with a gentle enough slope and sufficiently free of undergrowth to provide them a passable route to the cliffs.

"This looks as good a place as any," he said after a few minutes, and led them cross country.

Traversing in a northwesterly arc, they finally reached the massive wall, pale and grey in this light. There was an aura about the place; something mysterious. Or was it sinister? Aaron shivered.

He hoped to find a leveler surface to walk on once they arrived at the cliff's base, but it was not to be; they had to continue hurrying along on a slant.

As dusk approached, he heard his dad's voice bark from the radio.

"Come in Aaron. You read me?"

"Yeah, Dad." Aaron talked as he walked. "You're a little scratchy, but I read you okay."

"It's getting late. You need to be heading up."

"I know, but it will be a while before we reach the waterfall."

"Then come back up the shoulder."

"I think we can get to camp quicker if we just keep going. I'd say we're at least halfway."

The proposal was met by silence.

"Dad?"

"Okay, keep going. But don't waste any time. I don't want you down there after dark."

"Will do. How's Lena?"

"Lena? She's fine. A little rest and rehydration and she was good to go. She and her mom are with us now."

"Super. 10-4."

"Take care you two. See you soon."

Aaron could read between the lines. Finding Mr. Summerlin was no longer their top priority; getting back to camp as soon as possible was.

From somewhere the brothers summoned the energy to pick up speed. They didn't want to be caught out here after dark, either.

After about ten minutes more of this lopsided travel, Aaron veered away from the dark cliffs, hoping to make better time where the terrain was not so sloped.

"What about Mr. Summerlin?" Kyle asked.

"It's getting too dark to see much, anyway, and we need to speed it up."

They hadn't traveled far on this diagonal course when they crossed a gentle swale and dropped into what appeared to be an old, dry streambed. It afforded a fairly level surface, so they followed it.

Even though he doubted he could see anything from this distance, Aaron kept looking off to his right, in the direction of the cliffs, hoping he might spot something out of place.

After about fifteen minutes in the streambed, Aaron thought he saw the cliff through the trees. *Yes, I did.* They were angling toward it. *We're getting closer.*

Aaron checked their location on his GPS, thankful for its backlight. "Hey! Looks like we're almost to the waterfall. What say we finish up along the cliff?"

"If you can, I can."

They left their streambed sidewalk and made their way through the trees up a steadily increasing incline until they were a stone's throw from the cliff, where they resumed their parallel track. Back to walking on a slant, they hurried across the slope like a racing pair of peg-legged pirates.

Aaron no longer tried to scan the base of the cliff. Between the lack of light and the need to constantly watch one's feet, he found it hard enough just to stay upright. But it didn't stop him from worrying about what he was going to say to Lena.

"Owww!"

Aaron stopped and turned around to see Kyle on one knee. He was staring uphill at something while rubbing his right elbow.

Then Kyle's injured arm shot straight out. "Aar...Aar...Aaron!"

Aaron looked where Kyle was pointing, spotted the lump, and in an instant recognized the form. "Stay there!" he commanded, and rushed over to kneel beside the prostrate man.

The man was face down, with his head resting on his arm. One of his pant legs was torn and stained dark. The material felt stiff. *Dried blood.* Aaron shook his arm. He got no response but from its limpness Aaron guessed the man was still alive. He considered checking for a pulse, but his own heart was beating so hard he decided it was pointless to try.

Aaron turned to summon Kyle, but found that he was standing right behind him. Aaron thrust the handy-talky at him. "Here! Call Dad and tell him we've found Mr. Summerlin."

While Kyle radioed, Aaron tried to give the man some water but it ran down the man's cheek, across his partly opened lips, and pooled on the ground in front of his face. He didn't stir.

Kyle tapped him on the shoulder. "Dad wants to talk to you."

Aaron told his father as much as he could about the man's condition. "Oh, and Dad, he's wearing a climbing harness, and there's a pile of climbing rope down here."

"Explains why he's not...why his injuries aren't worse. What's your location?"

Aaron read him the GPS coordinates.

"Okay, sit tight and we'll get a SAR team down to you as soon as possible."

"Okay."

Aaron tried to think of what he could do in the meantime. He remembered the emergency blanket in his pack. Not much bigger than a deck of cards, it became a door-sized sheet of foil when opened up; gold on one side, silver on the other. *Flimsy thing, but maybe it'll do some good.* He draped it over the man.

After several minutes, the radio barked, "Aaron."

"Dad?"

"Yeah. How you two holding up?"

"We're fine." His voice was quavering. "A little nervous, I guess."

"Any change?"

"No, he's still not moving."

Arthur nodded. "Search and Rescue should be here before too long."

"I hope they hurry. He doesn't look too good."

"Can you check for ID without moving him?"

"I think so."

Aaron set down the radio, lifted the foil sheet, and carefully slid the man's wallet from his back pocket. He found the man's driver's license. He nodded to Kyle and then picked up the radio.

"Dad, it's Mr. Summerlin alright."

"Okay. We'll let Lena and her mother know. You two hang in there. I'll radio you when help gets here."

It was fully dark out before their father radioed to tell them that members of a search and rescue team had begun to filter into camp. At the news, the brothers gave each other a high-five, but time dragged on and still no one came. Aaron radioed to ask what was taking so long but all Arthur would say was that it took time to get things organized. He told him to be patient and not to radio him unless it was urgent.

To pass the time, Kyle came up with a new game, See Who Can Hit the Flashlight-lit Tree with a Rock. While they played, periodically Aaron would look over at Lena's father for any promising signs, but it seemed nobody was moving tonight.

Finally, the first responder rappelled down near their position. With impressive efficiency, the headlamp-wearing paramedic checked Mr. Summerlin's vital signs, inspected for injuries, gave him an injection, and hooked him up to a bag of intravenous fluid.

"How is he?" Aaron asked.

"Hard to say. Pulse is weak; probably dehydrated. Need to get his leg stabilized and get him to a hospital. If you hadn't found him when you did, well...."

Soon after this, Arthur radioed to say that he and Zach were hiking down to escort them out. They were to stay put until they got there. Aaron was about to protest that they could meet halfway, but he held his tongue. He figured his dad didn't need an argument right now.

Meanwhile, additional rescuers rappelled down one at a time. For a while, the brothers watched in fascination, but they grew frustrated as the SAR personnel debated at length how best to evacuate Mr. Summerlin. Aaron looked at Mr. Summerlin just lying there on the ground. *C'mon guys. Do something.*

"Aaron, look!" Kyle said in a loud whisper.

Beams of light were cutting through the forest from the south. It was creepy; like being in the midst of an alien invasion. Aaron looked over his shoulder, checking to be sure the SAR team members weren't deserting them.

After a tense few moments, Aaron relaxed when he recognized the invaders as John Colbert and several of his rangers. It relieved Aaron still further when Ranger Colbert took charge and announced that they would carry the injured man on a stretcher down to an access road where an ambulance would be waiting.

Suddenly, Aaron felt a hand grip his shoulder.

"Dad!"

Arthur had his other arm wrapped around Kyle, and he wore a huge smile.

"Good job guys," he said, drawing them tight to his chest. "I'm real proud of you."

CHAPTER 26
STATUS REPORTS

THEY WERE ABOUT HALFWAY to the trailhead when Zach stepped off the trail and sat down on a log bench. The Gardners followed his lead, glad for the chance to rest.

Had this trail been a highway, the spot surely would have been a scenic overlook. The sky retained a radiant navy blue tint above the wavy black profile of the southern range. A smattering of lights blinked meekly across the forested foothills. A domed glow marking Greenville radiated in the distance. But the best treat of all came when Zach and Arthur switched off their headlamps.

"Wow! I never knew there were so many stars!"

Aaron was as amazed as Kyle. Until now, had someone suggested that in a two-dimensional view there were more stars than empty sky Aaron would have said he was nuts.

"Isn't it something how they're there all the time but you wouldn't know it?" commented Zach.

"Yep, the darker it gets, the more the lights stand out," Arthur agreed.

"Dad, do you know what Lena and her mom plan to do now?" Aaron asked.

"You mean tonight? No I don't."

Zach did. "Big Mac said they were going…."

"Hah!" Kyle erupted.

"What's so funny? What'd I say?"

"Big Mac. That's a good one," Kyle explained.

"Yeah, that's what the staff call him. He's okay with it." Zach then turned to Aaron. "Anyway, the boss said the Summerlins were going to pack up and follow the ambulance to the hospital.

Aaron felt the air go out of him.

"You guys may have seen the last of Lena this trip," said Arthur.

Aaron did not want or need to hear this.

"Bummer, she was great," grumbled Kyle.

Aaron dropped his head. *This isn't the way it's supposed to be.* He had envisioned the four of them being swarmed by well-wishers as they came off of the trail. Lena would cut through the crowd, rush up to him and…and…*and now she won't be there? She's gone?* He kicked at a rock sticking out of the dirt.

Late that night, when the little company reached the road skirting the camp, all they saw were a few vehicles and a small cluster of men down the way; probably members of the SAR team waiting for their teammates to return. The weary foursome continued on to the dining hall, where they found director McIntyre waiting up for them, but that was the extent of their reception.

After that sobering look at the life of an everyday hero, a day of downtime, and a day spent exploring the cliff top in an attempt to piece together what Mr. Summerlin had been up to, the brothers went back to their routines. To Aaron, the days seemed drained of color.

And then Lena called.

She bubbled over with thanks for all they had done, told him she was sorry that she did not get a chance to say goodbye, and apologized for not calling sooner. She explained that for the first two days, they weren't sure if her father would make it. Now they expected him to pull through but feared he would lose his leg. He was still in an induced coma, she said.

Aaron did not like hearing the strain in her voice.

"Aaron, uh, I've wanted to ask…is it right what your father said; that you and Kyle went to look where you did because of the file and the map?"

"Yeah, we thought he might be searching for something over there."

"Do you know what?"

"Nope; only what Charlie said about rock hounds. How about you? You got any ideas?"

"I don't know anything." She sounded sad. "When we arrived at the hospital one of the rescuers handed us a belt thingy kind of like what we had at the ropes course. He said it was Daddy's."

Aaron nodded. "It's a climbing harness. Your dad was wearing it. There was climbing rope down there, too. And I guess the search and rescue guys found a bag of climbing gear at the top of the cliff. I don't know if they left it at the camp for your dad to pick up later, or what, but it's pretty clear he was rappelling along the cliff and the rope wore through."

"I…I don't understand. We learned about rappelling at the ropes course, but Daddy didn't seem to care. I don't think he knew anything about climbing and I didn't see any ropes or things like that in the car." Distress spilled from her voice. "Aaron, I wish I knew what was going on. So many secrets…."

"I wish I knew, too. Kyle and I talked about trying to find what your dad was looking for, but Mom vetoed the idea. She said we wouldn't even know it if we found it, but I think it's mostly 'cause of what happened to your dad. She never had a problem with us doing stuff like that before."

Aaron and Kyle were experienced rock climbers. A few years earlier Arthur had introduced them to the sport, steering them toward a rock climbing club which required novices to advance through a series of progressively more difficult climbs to win the right to tackle Looking Glass Rock, a huge lump of granite dropped in the middle of Pisgah National Forest outside of Brevard. With a near-vertical face as tall as a skyscraper, it was no place for beginners. The brothers took to the challenge and each already had several ascents and descents of the monolith under his climbing belt. In comparison, the cliffs below the camp would not be much of a challenge.

"When we go home I'm going to see what I can find," Lena decided aloud.

"Great! Maybe we can wear Mom down. And Lena, even if...if you just need somebody to talk to, I'm all ears." He pressed his knuckles against his forehead. *Sheesh. That was so lame.*

"Thank you, Aaron. That means a lot. I'll talk to you soon, and tell everybody 'hey' from me."

"Okay, bye."

"Bye."

Oh, that voice.

Less than a week later, Lena called again.

"Aaron, I found it!"

What Lena had found was Julisdanali's letter to Sadie. It was in her father's desk. She said that it explained everything, and by the time she finished giving Aaron the details, he was as excited as she.

"They didn't find any gold chunks or gold coins on your dad, did they?"

"No."

"I doubt he found the mine, then."

"Probably not, but it would have been nice if he did. I can see Mom's worried about how we're going to pay for everything now that Daddy's in the hospital. There may be something going on with his job, too. When we got home, there were some phone messages from them that upset her a lot."

"Is your dad out of his coma yet?"

"Oh, I'm sorry, didn't I tell you? Yes, and he's much better. He's even eating a little now."

"Can you ask him about it…the treasure, I mean?"

"Uh, well, I don't…uh…he kept it a secret and…uh…I don't know why, but I can't tell him that I know. I just can't. Uh, oh, I think Mom's home. I have to go. I'll call back soon. Bye."

She hung up before he could say goodbye but he shrugged it off and went to tell Kyle the news.

There was no stopping Kyle when he heard about the gold mine covered by a clay face in the side of the cliff. He launched a full scale assault upon the wall of Sandra's resistance. Twice she had to ask him to slow down as he regurgitated what he knew about the mine, the gold, and the coins. Aaron stood by to lend a nod or tweak the details. Arthur sat silently nearby, seemingly immersed in the Hendersonville newspaper.

That her sons would have a concrete goal seemed to open a crack in Sandra's resolve, but she did not break. It was too dangerous, she said; and besides, there was no telling how long ago that letter was written.

Aaron took a different approach. He told his mom about the Summerlins' money worries and about how finding the treasure would help. The wall of her resistance seemed to bend at this, but then she wondered aloud what right they had to be on that land and whether the Summerlins would even be entitled to the gold.

The brothers feared they had lost the battle and were about to retreat and regroup when Arthur set down the newspaper.

"Uh, hon, about that permission, I talked with Kelly McIntyre a week or so ago and he's given it the green light. And if you're worried that they might cross over into John's bailiwick, I'm sure he would tell the boys to go for it, but I'll touch base with him just to be sure."

Sandra said nothing for a time but just looked at him askance, as if wondering whose side he was on. Then she huffed: "Even if there really is a mine and even if they happen to find it, it wouldn't necessarily help the Summerlins."

"Maybe not," he replied, "but I don't see that as a reason not to let them give it a shot. We can worry about rights to the treasure if and when they find it. You know they're capable climbers, and they'll be careful, won't you boys?"

The brothers nodded like bobbleheads on the dashboard of a truck going down a washboardy road.

"And I'll leave them with a handy-talky so they can radio for help if they need it," Arthur added. "Kelly said either he or Zach would monitor the radio while the boys are on the cliff."

That did it. She caved. The mission was a go.

CHAPTER 27
FACE TO FACE

Five long days later

THE PLAN was to pick up where Mr. Summerlin left off. Having returned to explore the cliff top a couple of days after his rescue, they were confident he had been moving west, toward the waterfall. The trampled vegetation and pockets of litter he left behind told them as much. Since they couldn't rule out the possibility that the mine was in the section of the cliff above where he had fallen, they began there.

Although the brothers didn't know it, they opted to use the same make-like-a-pendulum technique as their predecessor. With the exception of a couple of items, their equipment was similar, too. They lacked an étrier but they did have something he didn't: a heavy canvas blanket to drape over the edge to protect the rope from chaffing. Their parents had made sure of it.

Having won the coin toss, Kyle went first and completed his inspection without incident. It was now Aaron's turn. Backing off a cliff always unnerved him, and he had to fight the dangerous urge to lean forward. It was only when his head dropped below the edge and he had a rock wall in front of him, that he grew calm; kind of like putting blinders on a horse.

Not wasting any time, he was soon rappelling down to where he would begin his third traverse. As he swung back into the cliff for a final push of his legs, Aaron focused on the wall in front of him.

"*Aaaagh!*" he screamed.

Staring him in the face was a wide mouthed, large lipped, dark faced man with jaundiced eyes and tobacco stained teeth.

"Aaron! You okay?" Kyle shouted, his head jutting beyond the edge.

After his heart stopped racing, Aaron looked up and shouted, "Yeah! Wait 'til you see this!"

"What?" Kyle shouted back.

"I found it!"

"Wahoo!"

Aaron pondered what to do. *If we tell Dad he may want to call in all sorts of experts. Zach and Mr. McIntyre would want to tell who knows who. We'll probably be shut out completely.* "Hmmm." Aaron slid his hand in his pocket and pulled out a small walky-talky (the brothers had brought a pair of the lightweight, short range devices so the two of them could communicate).

"Kyle, I think I'll try to cut it out, okay?"

A few moments later Kyle's voice crackled: "10-4."

"Could you send down the rock hammer and chisel in the drop bag?"

"Roger that."

Rolling his eyes at his brother's use of radio lingo, Aaron began to tie off the dead rope to free up both hands. Soon, gravel pelted his helmet—Kyle belaying the tools, he guessed—but he knew better than to look up to check on his progress. He kept his eyes front and hugged the wall, his head shielded by his helmet. But in his mind's eye he could see their prearranged plan go into action: Kyle had pushed the drop bag out from the cliff's edge using the "Y" shaped fork of a tree branch they had secured for this purpose and he was now standing on the branch while slowly releasing the slender nylon line through the branch's crotch.

However, the scene Aaron envisioned left out the part where Kyle realized he forgot to anchor himself to the tree, as he had at least twice assured Aaron he would do. Nor did it include Kyle's frantic attempts to lasso the tree without taking his foot off the branch.

Oblivious to such matters, all Aaron knew was that it was taking a long time for the bag to reach him, and this he attributed to his partner taking care not to conk him on the head with the tools. He had no inkling that Kyle was now paying out the line with reckless abandon.

While he patiently waited for the bag, Aaron inspected the face. It made a hollow sound when he rapped on it with his knuckles. He marveled at the yellowish whites of the eyes and the creepy teeth. *How had they been made to look so real?*

Suddenly, something flashed past his right shoulder. He spun away from it, banging his left side into the cliff wall. The object jerked to a stop at about the level of his waist, allowing him a glimpse of the tool bag, and then it shot down again.

Aaron whipped the radio to his mouth. "Whoa! You trying to kill me with that thing?"

Kyle tied the line to his harness then replied, "Sorry, I couldn't tell how far I needed to lower it."

"You went too far. You need to pull it up about twelve feet."

When the bag finally settled at the correct level, Aaron withdrew the tools and began to chip away at the mortar around the perimeter of the pottery face. Readily surrendering to the chisel, the mortar impressed him as weak, but a hard, unyielding, cement would have cracked and fallen away long ago.

It took Aaron about thirty minutes to complete the circuit. When he was done, he began to pry around the edge with his fingertips. It moved almost imperceptibly. He kept working at it, wiggling on one side and then the other, until he could get a good grip on the rim. Then he took a couple of deep breaths and tugged. The sculpted plate slid free; a lonely sentry finally relieved of duty.

Aaron rested the base of the clay visage across his thighs and peered over the top of its head. He could see a hole or recess in the cliff, but because his eyes were accustomed to the bright sunlight he could not tell how deep it was.

"Kyle, you still up there?"

"Yeah, who do you think is holding up the bag?"

Ignoring the question, Aaron asked him to pull up the drop bag and send down an empty rope bag.

"Didja get it out in one piece?"

"Yep."

"What's behind it?"

"There's a hole, but I can't see much yet."

Kyle got to work on making the exchange. The process went smoothly and within minutes Aaron had the face tucked into the rope bag. "Okay, are you ready to go for a little ride?" he asked as he zipped up the bag. Hearing no objection, Aaron toggled his radio.

"Ready, Kyle. Hoist away."

Aaron felt the weight being lifted off of him. The clay seal was in motion. He knew he wasn't supposed to look up, but he did it anyway. And once he saw it, he couldn't take his eyes off of it. Something about seeing the bag rise in a slow rotation was mesmerizing, like watching a scuba diver surfacing.

"Looks good, Kyle. You're doing great."

Aaron turned his attention to the hole in the wall. It was late enough in the day that he was now in the shadow of the cliff, which allowed his pupils to dilate some. He could see that the hollow was over a foot deep in places. He took out a small flashlight and shined it into the hole.

He gasped. A swath of glittering gold swept across the indentation. *Wow, wow, wow.* It looked like a retreating comet, its diffuse tail converging into a solid line as it neared the upper right corner. Aaron gazed at it for a time and then used the pliers of his Leatherman to break off a few small chunks.

He was about to put the flashlight away when something on the floor of the recess caught his eye. Nearly blending into the rock was a cloth sack, tied with thin corded strands. In his excitement, he'd almost forgotten about the coins.

The cloth was thin and discolored, reminding him of an old tea bag. He gently cradled the sack in his palm, fearing it may disintegrate. It wasn't very heavy; less than a pound, he guessed. The contents shifted in his hand. He was tempted to open it to confirm it held the coins, but decided not to risk it. He carefully slid it into one of his cargo pockets.

"Kyle, let me know when you've got your hands free," he radioed.

"Yo, bro; company's already here."

"Great. I've got some good news. I'll fill you in up top. You might get lunch ready in ten minutes or so."

"Roger that, but you better hurry. This guy looks a might hungry."

It took Aaron a few second to catch on. "Better not let him eat my half," he warned, only partly in jest.

"Not all of it," assured the one with the literally upper hand.

Knowing a reply would only serve to egg his brother on, Aaron put away the radio. He reached for the ascenders but then paused to shine the flashlight across the golden band one more time.

If this is really gold...man...oh, man. Wait 'til I tell Lena!

CHAPTER 28
JOY IN THE JOURNEY

Summer's end

THE GARDNERS had crossed into Georgia from South Carolina about an hour before and were now sprinting toward Atlanta on the Interstate. Aaron stared blindly out the car window, mulling over how quickly things can change.

Arthur had suggested they not say anything to Lena about their discovery until they confirmed it was really gold and until after he consulted a lawyer friend in Hendersonville, so Aaron had kept quiet.

It hadn't been easy, and it got even harder after Charlie examined the samples. Charlie said they would need to check with an assayer to be sure, but the look on his face told the story. It was gold all right. Aaron couldn't wait to tell her.

Then Arthur reported on his meeting with the lawyer. It sounded like the Summerlins wouldn't get the gold. The news soured Aaron's mood big time, and he had to force himself to make the call to Lena.

He could still hear the disappointment which bled from her voice. "Aaron, I gave you that letter so you could help Daddy. I counted on you." That had hurt. *Maybe if I told her how hard I fought Dad over this*. But he knew that it would not make things any better for the Summerlins, so he kept it to himself.

He figured she must have realized he felt bad about it, too, because by conversation's end she seemed her usual warm self. But now he was beginning to worry that her apparent change of heart had only been an act. Two weeks had passed and he hadn't heard from her. He was *really* looking forward to seeing her and was glad their mothers had arranged this get together, but not knowing what kind of reception he would receive made him a nervous wreck.

His internal adviser was hard at work. *Man, don't get so uptight. This probably is the last time you'll see her; it's silly to get so worked up. Chill, be cool. Just be a friend.* All good arguments. All equally ineffective.

It didn't help that they were making this trip during his last weekend of freedom. Even though his head knew he would really like it once he got into the routine, his gut always dreaded the start of school.

Aaron could tell that he wasn't the only one feeling punk. From the way his dad was rubbing the back of his neck and pressing against his temple, he guessed he had a severe headache, and Kyle was a curious shade of green.

Arthur was suffering from the traffic, which had turned into a mad rush as they neared the city. As for Kyle, well, Aaron felt a little bad about that. Despite Kyle's protests, he had bought a bag of boiled peanuts at a roadside stand back in South Carolina. The odor always seemed to turn Kyle's stomach—although Aaron couldn't fathom why.

When their car squirted onto an off-ramp, Aaron's case of nerves progressed to the jittery quivers.

Only his mom seemed her usual self. Aaron really hoped that when they reached the Summerlins she would be able to cover for them a while.

He needn't have worried. As the crazy traffic abated, so did Arthur's tension. The slower speeds allowed them to roll down the windows and air out the car, which quickly cured Kyle's affliction. And by the time they turned onto Lena's street, Aaron's once-galloping heartbeat had turned to a prance.

When his dad pulled into the driveway of a house with a "For Sale" sign in the yard, Aaron at first thought they were at the wrong address. Lena hadn't said anything about selling their house. But then she bounced out the front door, waving like crazy.

Without thinking, he jumped out of the car and met her at the edge of the driveway. Before he had time to say anything, she had wrapped her arms around his waist and pressed her head against his chest.

"Aaron, I'm so glad you're here."

He stood there awkwardly for a moment, his arms dangling. He was about to hug her back when she danced over to give hugs to the rest of his family.

She's not mad at me after all. Aaron was ecstatic.

He turned and saw that Mrs. Summerlin had come out onto the veranda. Mr. Summerlin, cane in hand, stood in the doorway. His face seemed softer than he remembered. Both were smiling. Aaron hesitatingly took a step in their direction but then stopped and waited for his parents to take the lead.

Soon, he was sandwiched in a procession led by his mom and dad. Kyle and Lena brought up the rear, hip-bumping each other off the walkway.

The Summerlins seemed genuinely happy to see them. After receiving a gentle, warm handshake from Lena's mother, Aaron stepped over the threshold and found himself in the grip of Lena's father.

"Let me give my rescuers a big hug!" their host requested somewhat belatedly.

Aaron just stood there crumpled up with a crooked grin on his face.

"Kyle, come on up here," the man commanded.

Kyle crept tentatively forward. When he was in reach, the man wrapped him up in his free arm.

"I owe my life to you two," he said, his voice low and serious. He gave Kyle another good squeeze and then announced, "Now, let's go get us some Georgia swamp water!"

Huh? Aaron looked at Kyle and could tell that he was at a loss, too.

Shepherded by their hobbling host, they entered the living room just as the mothers and Lena were walking into the kitchen. Mr. Summerlin had Arthur and the brothers take a seat and asked about the trip down. Aaron tuned out the conversation and repeatedly glanced through the nearby doorway to catch glimpses of Lena moving about the kitchen. He tried not to look too obvious.

Shortly, the women returned, carrying trays bearing slices of dessert breads, a pitcher and seven glasses filled with a dark sludgy liquid.

Aaron chuckled inwardly when he saw Kyle staring dubiously at his glass. He could guess what Kyle was thinking: *First boiled peanuts, and now this!* The waters of Georgia's famed Okefenokee Swamp were nearly black with tannin from all the rotting vegetation. Aaron suspected this was what gave the drink its color, but why Georgians would drink from it, he hadn't a clue.

"Hmmm, this is great, Linda," said Arthur, licking his lips. "What's in it?"

"Oh, it's made with iced tea, peach nectar, of course, and then I toss in some berries and pieces of fruit; whatever is handy. I keep my recipe a secret by constantly changing it."

Arthur smiled back. "Well, whatever recipe you used, it worked."

Kyle dared a sip, and a look of pleasant surprise washed over his face.

Arthur turned to Grady. "It was great to hear that your leg is on the mend."

"Yeah, Art, it's healing on schedule, I'm told. Another couple of months and I should be able to walk without a cast, or at least trade this brute for a shorter and lighter one."

"The doctor said he may always have to use a cane, though; it was a very bad break," Linda inserted.

Grady nodded. "I've got enough metal in me I probably won't ever get through an airport. But it's a lot better than never walking again, and I owe it all to you good folks."

"And to a daughter who remembered you having a file like the one the boys found. It's what led them to search where they did," Arthur noted.

Grady nodded while looking fondly at Lena.

"Lena was like one of the family," Sandra added. "We were glad to do what we could to help."

Aaron leaned toward Lena and whispered, "Why are you moving?" Although he had tried to keep his voice down, it was obvious everyone had heard. The question hung in the air. *What did I do wrong?* Aaron wondered.

Lena looked beseechingly at her parents.

Grady answered for her. "Those medical folks are mighty proud of their work. Even the supplies are ridiculous. Had I known it would cost so much to blow my nose, I would have used dollar bills."

"Now, Grady, they took good care of you, and you know it," Linda scolded.

He just smiled at her and continued. "Anyway, even though I had insurance, it didn't pay for everything. And on top of that I was fired from my job, so I've got no salary coming in. Between the medical bills and mortgage we can't begin to cover our expenses, so we decided it was time to scale down."

Looking at her husband tenderly, Linda reached over and put her hand on his leg. Grady covered her hand with his and returned her smile.

Kyle was incredulous. "Can they fire you when you're laid up?"

"I don't know what the law is, Kyle, but the company doesn't have many employees and they can't afford to pay for someone who isn't producing; and to tell you the truth, I hadn't been pulling my weight for a long time before the accident. I had it coming."

"You seem to be handling it pretty well, Grady," Arthur said. "I doubt most folks would stay so positive in the face of all this."

Grady leaned forward, rested his forearms on his thighs, and clasped his hands together like a child forming a church steeple. Then he looked up at Arthur. "You know, I've thought the same thing myself," he began. "That fall may have been the best thing that ever happened to me. I don't look at things the same way now. Used to be, the almighty dollar was numero uno. Not anymore. It's not that it's unimportant. I guess I just feel I have a better perspective. To have a wife that loves me; to look into the eyes of my daughter." Grady's voice wavered and tears welled in his eyes, but after a couple of deep breaths he sat up straight and went on.

"I can't explain it, but I was laying there in the dark and looked up and saw more stars than I had ever seen in my life. I started to feel more at peace; like I'd been sent a message. It couldn't be just one lucky accident that we're here; that so many things came together to make this earth a perfectly habitable place. I felt small, but my problems seemed small, too. I don't know if it was fatalism or what, but I knew if whoever put this all together wanted me to die, that's what would happen. And if He wanted me to live, I would. It was out of my hands." He turned his hands palm up to demonstrate his helplessness.

"Next thing I knew," he continued, "I was waking up in a hospital in Greenville and hearing about my two guardian angels, here." At this, he smiled and gestured toward Aaron and Kyle. "Ever since, I've been counting my blessings and trusting something or Someone greater than myself."

At the mention of guardian angels, Kyle took a brief break from his new game of Swing Your Foot Back and Forth to See How Many Times You Can Knock the Toe of Lena's Shoe.

"Grady, we came here to bring you some big news, but now it doesn't seem nearly so important." Arthur lowered his eyes momentarily and then looked up at his host. "I'm almost afraid to tell you lest it mess up a good thing."

"After what we've been through, I figure we can stand it," Grady said with a grin. "Go ahead and hit me."

Kyle quit pestering Lena and scooted forward. He and Aaron smiled at each other. *It's about time!*

"Well, we've come to tell you about Julisdanali's treasure."

CHAPTER 29
SOARING EAGLES

"*YOU FOUND IT?*" Grady shouted.

Linda and Lena jumped and Kyle laughed.

Arthur nodded. "Yes, the boys did."

"But how?" Grady stared at the table. He looked more stunned than pleased.

"Well, you probably know Lena found the old map there in your cabin. We figured you must have had something that told you more about it and what the drawing of the face meant. While you were still in the hospital Lena found the letter and she told the boys."

"I should have guessed," Grady nodded. "The letter's the only way you could have known the man's name." He immediately turned to Linda and asked, "But why didn't you tell me?"

"We wanted to let the Gardners surprise you," she answered.

I wouldn't have wanted to tell him either, thought Aaron.

Suddenly Lena blurted, "I'm sorry about getting into your papers, Daddy. I had to know what was going on and I didn't know what else to do."

"That's okay, honey, I understand."

Linda asked to hear more.

When Arthur got to the part where Aaron came eye to eye with the face seal, Grady spoke up, his voice matter of fact, "It was really there, huh?"

"Yep," said Aaron. "And it came out in one piece!"

Grinning, Arthur went on. "The camp's board of directors has agreed to donate the face to the Folk Art Center which, if you're not familiar with it, is just east of Asheville along the Blue Ridge Parkway."

"The Center's curator plans to schedule a public unveiling," Sandra added. "And Aaron and Kyle have been asked to speak."

Kyle seemed eager. Aaron wasn't.

"Aaron, do you want to tell us what you found inside?" Arthur invited.

Aaron perked up. "Sure. There were some gold coins in an old cloth bag and I saw a lot of shiny yellow specks in the wall of the cave."

"The camp had a sample assayed," noted Arthur. "It is gold. High grade. And there's quite a bit of it, I understand."

"Who's going to get it?" asked Grady, his voice dry and tight.

Lena and her mother looked at each other nervously. Aaron dropped his eyes.

"An attorney friend told me that the raw gold most likely belongs to the landowner, which is the organization that runs that camp you attended."

"Huh," Grady exhaled, "I would have thought you all would get it; 'finders keepers,' you know."

Arthur shook his head. "The lawyer didn't think so, and I've already met with the camp's board to assure them that we don't plan to make any claim, but we—the camp's director and I—did propose they do something to honor Julisdanali as sort of a finder's fee, and they agreed. I think you'll be pleased."

Probably about as pleased as we were, thought Aaron, recalling how he and Kyle felt when they learned they weren't getting anything out of the deal. He really wished his dad would have started with the coins.

As if he had read Aaron's mind, Arthur added, "But before I get to that, let me fill you in on the coins."

Aaron slid forward in his seat and Kyle started rocking back and forth on his hands.

"The bathroom is down the hall," Linda mouthed to Kyle, gesturing with her hands to show him the way.

Kyle just smiled and stayed put.

"Since they're personal property," Arthur began, "the lawyer said that heirs of Julisdanali's sister, Sadie, would have the strongest claim. He looked into it and believes that Linda and Lena are her last living descendants. We've spoken to the camp's board about it, and everybody's in agreement that the coins should go to them." As he said it, he stretched out one arm toward Lena and the other toward Linda.

Their faces immediately lit up, but Grady wore the expression of one who had just been awarded the consolation prize. Aaron guessed that he remembered what Julisdanali had written about the coins.

"How many are there?" Lena asked excitedly.

"Your turn, Kyle" said Arthur with a smile.

Kyle had inventoried the coins no less than three times in the hours after the discovery, carefully placing them in little piles by denomination. The self-appointed accountant gladly shared his findings.

"There were three eagles, four half eagles and seven quarter eagles."

"An eagle is a $10 gold coin," Aaron explained.

"So fourteen coins with a face value of about...fff..uh...sss..." Grady struggled with the math.

"$67.50," Kyle declared helpfully.

Grady slumped over like a boxer who had gone nine rounds. He stifled a groan when Arthur asked Aaron to tell the group what had been learned about the coins.

"Charlie Barnes, a friend of ours who works with Dad, knows a lot about coins and he looked into it for us," Aaron began. He found they were made by Templeton Reid, a German immigrant who opened his own mint in Georgia after gold was discovered there in the early 1800's."

Linda Summerlin looked surprised.

"He wasn't in business very long, though," Aaron continued. "Someone wrote a letter to the newspaper claiming his coins didn't contain enough gold, and even though Mr. Reid claimed this wasn't true, merchants wouldn't accept them. So most of the coins he made were sent to the U.S. Mint in Philadelphia to be melted down and made into new coins."

Aaron looked at his dad to signal that it was time for him to take over. The subject made Aaron nervous, and, besides, his dad had kept the latest information about the coins to himself.

Kyle was really rocking now.

"Promise me you won't faint folks," said Arthur, accepting the handoff. "Charlie told us that in 1979 a single Reid half-eagle was sold for $200,000."

Grady and Linda Summerlin gasped and drew together on the sofa where they sat in wide-eyed silence, their hands clutched tightly together in a ball. Lena's upper body jutted forward as she drew her legs up under her seat and jammed her prayerful hands between her knees. Apparently realizing how silly she must look with her mouth wide open like that of a hungry baby bird, she bit her lower lip.

Kyle, however, burst out laughing, and the rest of the Gardners were all smiles, too.

"Hold on; there's more," continued Arthur after a moment. "Charlie referred us to a company that specializes in rare coins—that's where your coins are now, by the way. Their expert said that until your coins showed up, it was thought that only a half a dozen Reid golden eagles survived, and not many more half eagles."

When had Mr. and Mrs. Summerlins' lips begun to quiver, Aaron wondered?

"He also tells me that a set of the three denominations of Reid coins came up for auction a few years ago." Arthur paused to look each member of his rapt audience in the eyes and then dropped the hammer. "The set brought over a *million*."

"No way!" Kyle shouted. Lena just squeaked. Her mother had her hand over her mouth and started to cry. Grady was fighting not to do the same. A moment or two later and Sandra's eyes were flowing, too. Aaron and Arthur just chuckled.

"And he said your coins…." Arthur, now wearing a smile nearly as wide as his face, gave them another few seconds to return him their attention. "Your coins are in such good condition that if you were to offer a three-coin set today, he thinks it could bring *twice* that."

Kyle exploded out of his chair, threw up his arms like a referee signaling a touchdown, and hollered, "You can buy the hospital!"

Arthur motioned for Kyle to sit down, and then added: "If you were to offer Julisdanali's letter with the entire collection, apparently the sky's the limit."

At this, Lena launched herself over to the couch to join her parents in what Aaron judged to be the most tearful happy family hug he had ever seen.

CHAPTER 30
HOMEWARD BOUND

AARON CONCLUDED that a restaurant parking lot was a lousy place to say goodbye.

It had been more than an hour since the Gardners had left for home but Aaron had sat silently the entire time, mostly looking out the side window and daydreaming about Lena, or, more specifically, Lena on their way to dinner.

It had started when Grady broke from their family huddle with a clap of his hands and announced that it was a time to celebrate; the Summerlins were taking the Gardners to "the best barbeque joint this side of Kansas City." And this was how Aaron *finally* got to ride next to Lena; him on one side, Kyle on the other, together in the back seat of the Summerlins' car.

Aaron had gotten his wish without a bit of finagling. It was purely a fortuitous event, some would say: a by-product of Grady's broken leg and the Gardners being strangers to the area. Grady required a back seat to stretch out on and the Gardners needed a navigator, so it was decided that Grady would ride with Arthur in one car while Sandra and three teens accompanied Linda in the other.

Aaron could still picture the look on Lena's face when he climbed in. She had smiled at him before, of course, but this time it was different. He got all squishy inside. Too, he could still feel the soft heat of her bare leg as it brushed against his—such glorious torture.

But the reflections were bittersweet. The thought he may never see her again was killing him.

Arthur seemed clueless, but Sandra knew he was suffering and eyed him sympathetically. Kyle, too, could tell he was in pain, so naturally he began to tease him about missing his girlfriend; a questionable move which caused Aaron's focus to suddenly shift from the window to his little brother's eyeballs. Kyle knew that look and backed off.

It wasn't too long after they crossed into South Carolina that Sandra saw a sign marking the Cherokee Foothills Scenic Highway. It dawned on her that they had neglected to tell the Summerlins about the scholarships and the Cherokee Heritage Camp the camp's Board agreed to offer. She mentioned it to Arthur.

Kyle cut in. "What's that?"

"Cherokee Heritage Camp? They're going to set aside a week where campers will learn about the Cherokee peoples," Arthur explained. "Maybe play stick ball, make masks, use blowguns…."

Blowguns? Worry creased Sandra's forehead.

"Blowguns! Cool! Can I go?" Kyle demanded to know.

"We'll see," answered Arthur with a grin. Then he looked over at Sandra and said, "Remind me to tell them when they come up to hear the boys give their presentation at the Folk Art Center."

The seemingly innocuous remark sparked all sorts of reactions. Aaron suppressed a smile and started to plan his speech. Wide-eyed Kyle immediately wondered aloud whether it would be too late in the season to take Lena to Sliding Rock.

Forehead furrowed, Sandra interrogated Arthur about when Grady had told him they were coming and why he hadn't bothered to share the news sooner.

Before long, however, they all were enjoying the scenery as they weaved and bobbed their way through upcountry South Carolina, an area rife with place names like Tokeena and Oconee; names that told that native peoples once considered this their homeland.

"Look, a town called Walhalla!" said Kyle, pointing at a road sign. "There's a place called 'Valhalla' in Norse mythology. It's kind of like heaven. Do you think Norsemen could have made it this far inland?"

"Good question," replied Arthur. "My guess is that Walhalla is a Cherokee word and that the similarity is coincidental, but it might make for interesting research."

"That reminds me of the speaker who came to the library last week to talk about Cherokee legends," recalled Sandra. "He said that one tells of monsters a lot like those in *Beowulf*, an old poem based on ancient Scandanavian lore."

"What *kind* of monsters?" Kyle was all ears.

"The one I remember best is Spear-finger," answered Sandra, her voice growing sinister. "She would use her bony forefinger to stab her victims and rip out their livers." Sandra scrunched an eye and wiggled her finger with the telling. And when she said "livers", she popped her finger into her mouth, chewed on something a bit, and then licked her lips with an "Mmmm."

The demonstration made Aaron not a little uncomfortable. He looked over at Kyle and saw him eyeing the passenger in the front seat closely, as if he, too, was wondering who the strange woman was.

Reverting to the mother they knew, Sandra continued. "She supposedly lived in a cave on Whiteside Mountain not too far north of where we are now. And get this: in the mid-1800's a man wrote about a cave in that mountain which could only be reached by a narrow, dangerous trail from the mountaintop. Inside, there was a huge tree trunk; one so big no human could have carried it there. The speaker wondered if Spear-finger might have hauled the tree to her lair for firewood."

"What's even stranger," she added, pausing to glare at Arthur for punctuating her account with eerie sound effects, "...what's even stranger, today nobody knows how to find the cave."

"*Cool,*" said Kyle, who then locked eyes with Aaron. The brothers nodded to one another.

Just as he turned his eyes back to the road, Aaron saw a sign for the produce stand they had stopped at that morning. The muscles in his neck tightened at the thought his mother might see it and "suggest" that they stop—"she never met a fruit stand she didn't like," his dad would say.

His dad must have spotted it, too, because Aaron could feel the car slowing. But then it speeded up again. The rustic, roadside establishment was unlit and shuttered for the night.

"Oh, he's closed," Sandra sighed.

"Darn," said Arthur unconvincingly.

Seeing the stand reminded Aaron of the snacks Sandra had packed for the trip.

"Any grapes left, Mom?" he asked.

"I think so," she answered, passing the cooler to him over the seat.

Aaron had just lifted the lid when a dark blur out of nowhere darted inside. The quick, unexpected thrust paralyzed Aaron and allowed Kyle to escape with a bunch of the juicy orbs.

Several loosely affixed spheres dropped to the floor and scattered, as if running for their lives.

Kyle undid his safety belt and dove for them. Aaron watched him reach under the passenger seat, fish around a bit, and then look up at him with a curious look on his face.

"Hah!" he cried, and drew out his find from under the seat.

"What?" Arthur asked.

"That's where it was," said Aaron.

Kyle scooted forward and reached over the seat, holding the object out as if he were offering his parents a bite from a Popsicle.

"There it is. I wondered where that ol' ba…."

"Ar*thur*," Sandra censored.

The brothers just grinned.

THE END

ACKNOWLEDGMENTS

Writing a novel and getting it published can be a big chore. I would not have been able to see it through without the support of my long-suffering spouse. Thanks hon.

The Helmans and YMCA Camp Greenville played an early part, although neither they nor I knew it at the time. Their gracious hospitality afforded me the opportunity to become acquainted with this beautiful part of the country.

Special thanks are also due to Colleen Aagesen whose advice to "show, not tell" proved most constructive, and to Diane Alden for her constant encouragement.